This book is dedicated to my wife,
and all my other friends too.

First printing

At the specific preference of the author, PublishAmerica allowed
this work to remain exactly as the author intended, verbatim,
without editorial input.

ISBN: 1-4137-9324-X
PUBLISHED BY PUBLISHAMERICA, LLLP
www.publishamerica.com
Baltimore

Printed in the United States of America

F

PublishAmerica
Baltimore

CONTENTS

1. The Big Debate

Credit: www.headstartproject.org

A once carefree planet, with its distinctive globe of swirling white clouds and deep blue oceans drifted through the black vacuum, circling about a yellow star called the Sun. Its serene outward appearance of course concealed from view the true scale of catastrophic climate change, deadly diseases and complete technological collapse that presently loomed before its inhabitants.

On May 1st, 2250, senior representatives from the world's highest ranking authorities gathered at the Global Space Agency headquarters in Washington D.C. to conclude the Big Debate that had been raging for decades.

In the first thirty minutes there was no clear consensus either way, as opinion still seemed divided between the financial burden of building such a large scale starship on the one hand against the potential risks if we lost our spaceflight capabilities in the impending global disasters, on the other.

The US president, Joseph Lexington sat on a highly elevated row of seats at the back of the briefing hall alongside other top officials from the United Nations, World Bank and the World Health Organisation, who were all listening intently to the raging debate.

A rather tall, slim man with greasy black hair and wearing a governmental suit rushed into the briefing hall via one of the doors on the upper level of the auditorium. He took brisk steps to walk over to the president and seemed short of breath, as if he'd been running a marathon.

'Sir, all hell is breaking loose out there and we're calling an emergency press conference,' he said in a highly urgent voice.

'You mean the status of the South African blizzards?' Lexington replied, in a half whisper.

'No sir, it's a lot worse. A tidal wave along the Pacific rim has reportedly wiped out two hundred thousand in eastern China - just in the past hour, sir.'

Lexington turned to the distinguished guests sat beside him, made a brief gesture asking to be excused and left the auditorium in a hurry.

Meanwhile, the debate continued to rage for the next two and a half hours.

Lexington's eldest son, Sebastian, had accompanied a climate study survey team to South Africa in an effort to closely monitor the Antarctic chilled stream that now devastated the region. Fully equipped with a mobile habitat, two military helicopters and ample expedition supplies, the eight-man crew had been stationed west of Johannesburg, on the southern edge of the Kalahari desert. Where the ground was once a large, arid to semi-arid desert covered in reddish brown sands for as far as the eye could see, on this night *it stood under four feet of snow.*

The blizzards had been raging violently and non-stop for the past three days, and the men longed for a break. On this night the break had finally arrived, with the skies clearing from the west shortly after sunset. The full moon cast its brilliant silver light onto the white blanket of snow, and the landscape looked intensely dazzling for miles around.

'Hey you guys, I'm going out to get some night air,' Sebastian said to two of his team mates.

'At this hour? Man, I'd keep an eye out for the hyenas if I were you,' one of them replied, half jokingly.

'No sweat. I've got this,' Sebastian said, pointing to the ray gun in his trouser pocket.

He was wrapped up warm in a hooded fur coat, padded with several layers underneath for insulation against the sub zero temperatures.

Having walked a fair distance away from the cabin, he stood out in the sea of freshly fallen snow, admiring the surrounding night scene. Screams from a pack of spotted hyenas echoed through the forests in the distance. They were too far away to pose any immediate threats, he thought.

Looking toward the west, he saw masses of fluffy white clouds race their way across the face of the moon, in the sweeping breeze. Shifting his gaze higher up toward the southern sky, he found a rather bright yellowish-looking star, not far from the group of four bright stars that made up the well known constellation of Crux, the 'Southern Cross'.

As he stood admiring the night sky, Sebastian heard the sound of boots crunching their way into deep snow behind him. Turning around, he felt somewhat relieved to see the leader of the survey team coming over to join him.

'Alpha Centauri. The third brightest star in our night sky,' the man said, peering toward the twinkling gem that had caught Sebastian's eye.

'It's hard to believe that small point of light is currently the focus of so much attention the whole world over.'

'Oh, absolutely. It always has been to some degree, although never as much as now. And your father has every confidence the Big Debate is going to conclude in his favour, enabling him to fulfil his grand vision.'

Back at the Global Space Agency headquarters, the atmosphere inside the auditorium had turned intensely agitating, in a somewhat bitter political battle fought with words; agendas were widely divided and minds filled with suspicion.

'Look, we see all these problems coming our way and yet we just sit around and do *nothing*?' Said a proponent of the cosmic ark proposal.

'The political will simply isn't there. Countries in the far east just do not share your optimism for this project, they have far more pressing problems to deal with at home,' said an opponent.

'I say screw the far easterners. Beyond the Earth, we have searched every corner of our own solar system and so far we've found nothing more advanced than a few microbes swimming in the oceans of Europa. The nearest place beyond the confines of our home planet that has breathable air, is located at a comfortable distance from its parent star with oceans of liquid water, and in all probability is teeming with proper life, is New Earth at Alpha Centauri. I see *that* as a logical next target for permanent human settlement,' remarked a rather knowledgeable proponent.

'Yeah, only it's going to take at least 50,000 years to reach that pinprick of light! Besides, have you considered the *true* financial cost of building such a gigantic vessel? It would be no less than the total world GDP multiplied by a factor of god knows how much,' remarked one of the opponents. 'Would you just look at the size of that thing!' He said, chuckling whilst pointing to a 3D graphical animation of the giant, would-be starship played back on a video screen in one corner of the meeting hall. He was a senior official of the Chinese High Empire.

Maxine Hathaway was feeling pretty uptight by now, and weary from all the hours of sitting there listening to such mind-rotting rubbish; her patience wearing a little thin. *Are all of these people really so blind to the situation?* Joseph Lexington was relying on *her* courage, more so than anyone else's, to make the distinguishing mark that would settle this whole thing once and for all.

She adjusted the volume level of the microphone clipped to her blouse. Here it goes, she thought, talking into the device.

'Costs and finances? The world is falling apart and we

are still talking about money. That's just pitiful. Hey, an original Picasso painting is worth two hundred million dollars at an average auction in New York City these days. That's the going rate for a piece of vanity art that's going to rest on the wall of some fat cat's penthouse suite. May I point out that that same painting's worth of dollars would prolong the lives of five thousand refugees in eastern Europe suffering from AIDS by no less than ten long god damn years, and still leave plenty spare to fight the current epidemic of skin cancer over here. You still don't see just how arbitrary and disproportionately skewed our financial systems are, do you? I ask everyone gathered here today, is there any price high enough worth paying to save the human race from extinction? I'm not talking about me gaining a promotion or you gaining a salary increase here. No, I'm talking about your children, my children, our children's children…the future of our entire god damn species.'

Faces of opponents all around the auditorium had a look of disbelief that someone from the younger generation, in her late twenties, could make such a bold and profound statement. She continued:

'No one gathered here today will oppose the wisdom established by science with regards to the likely evolutionary route our species has taken since the humble beginnings of life on our planet as micro-organisms in a primitive ocean some four billion years ago. We eventually crawled out of that ocean, developing in stages to dominate the planet as conscious, self aware, intelligent beings with hopeful futures and pleasant dreams. We looked up at the night sky in wonder, and saw billions of stars with potentially habitable zones around each of them and noted so many extra-solar planets in our journals. We developed technology to take us to the Moon and onwards even further out to Mars and had every potential to reach for the immensely distant stars.'

She paused for breath and took a sip of mineral water from the glass in front of her.

'Suppose now, through one of the many well known dangers facing our planetary cradle, our species is destroyed right here on Earth where it was born, before we had the opportunity to launch a single part of human society to safety on one of the countless far off worlds we see glittering across our night sky. How much of a tragedy would that look from a universal standpoint?'

That last statement appeared to have drummed home a touching message, making the briefing hall unusually silent for a long ten seconds.

A round of applause followed, prompted by a senior official of the US Pentagon who was visibly impressed by these remarks. He was a ginger haired man, with a cold face styled with black rimmed glasses and dressed in the Pentagon's military uniform.

'Dr. Hathaway has made some interesting points here which ring true, certainly to my mind. As far as we know, ours is the only planet in the entire god damn universe where life has evolved to this height and it's in all of our best interests to revere that fact. This may be the very last window of opportunity left to us. If we launch for Alpha Centauri now, a future generation will have a fighting chance to prevail and continue the onward propagation of humanity through the vastness of our galaxy, in the aeons of time that stretch before us.'

Eventually, a voting session of all those in favour compared to all those against the starship proposal, showed the tide of public opinion to be overwhelmingly in favour of the proponents. A follow-up council meeting held on May 20th, 2250 gave the Global Space Agency go ahead and funding for an orbital engineering program spanning twenty five years. That was to culminate in the construction of the giant ark ship - dubbed the *'Centauri Princess'* - which would eventually take a section of our planet and people to New Earth, an Earth-like planet located in the habitable zone around one of the stars of the Alpha Centauri triple star system.

The 'funding' granted by the world authorities to the Global Space Agency, mentioned above, was no funding on a scale that could be measured in the conventional monetary sense at all. It was basically limitless amounts of economically unmeasured materials, machines and manpower - whatever it took - for planet Earth's last technologically advanced civilisation to build the last, the only, interstellar ark to safeguard its long term survival. The program focussed the undivided attention and efforts of ten billion people the whole world over; the sum of every last hope…every last fighting breath,…the pooling together of every last ounce of knowledge from every last one of the world's finest minds that ever were and ever had been.

And why did the vessel take as long as twenty five years to build? Well, the program's project teams had envisioned that to be a reasonable timescale in order to bring together all of the necessary components, from as far a field as factories operating in orbit around the Moon and locations in the asteroid main belt. Those components were then supplemented by hardware developed here on Earth, to construct something in high Earth orbit on a technological scale that was to eclipse all other prior engineering achievements in all human history.

New Earth itself was first detected by NASA's Earth-circling *Terrestrial Planet Finder* mission back in the mid-twenty first century. That discovery was immediately hailed as the greatest extra-solar system insight to have been ever acquired in the entire history of science. Advanced spectroscopic studies from the Lunar Far Side Observatory later revealed the planet to be virtually a near-twin of our own Earth, with oceans of water, a breathable nitrogen/oxygen atmosphere, and clear evidence of some seasonally changing vegetation.

If granting mankind the ability to identify New Earth on the nearest cosmic shores beyond our solar system were to be god's way of showing us an avenue of escape to aim for, then he certainly had set the challenge extremely steeply indeed. Alpha Centauri is a little over four light years from Earth. This may not sound that great a distance in the vastness of the wider cosmos, but translated into every day measure, the nearest island of light beyond our Sun is a staggering 25,000,000,000,000 (twenty five million million) miles away across the vast interstellar ocean of darkness stretching out beyond the orbit of Pluto...

2. Last link with the cradle

Credit: NASA-Apollo 17

Credit: www.headstartproject.org

The north polar ice sheets had continued to edge their way south and reached as far down as southern Europe, since the start of the Great Ice Age two thousand years earlier. In that period, just over half of the world population had been wiped out through disease, cold and deprivation.

Presently, the surviving communities huddled together in warmer tropical regions like Central America and Africa, where life was just about tolerable. Space technological capabilities had been diminished into obscurity compared to the great heights of the late twenty third century, with just two rocket launch sites in the jungles of French Guiana in South America, still operational.

Nestled away, amid the deep rain forests in a jungle location in Central America, a team of four people had been trying to establish communications with the *Centauri Princess* starship, now sailing approximately eleven thousand five hundred astronomical units from the Sun (one trillion miles from Earth). Despite all the calamities that the planet had undergone in the past two thousand years, with the ever changing fortunes of civilisations across the globe, keeping an ongoing link and synchronised communications protocol with the starship after such an astonishing time span, was perhaps the greatest outcome that anyone could ever have hoped for.

Presently though, looking over a log of auto-transmission attempts over the past six weeks, the communications team saw a series of random noise pulses in the return signals received from the ship, due to lack of power on the dilapidated interstellar telecom equipment at the Earth-end of the link.

'They are all on their own now,' said one of the telecom engineers in a rather downbeat tone.

Subsequent to this, no further telecom link could be made with the starship. Our distant descendants, who were carrying with them all the hopes and dreams of the entire human race on this epic first voyage out into the eternity of space, had phoned home quite possibly for the very last time...

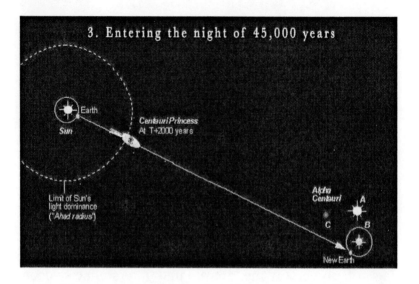

3. Entering the night of 45,000 years

In this era, in the final year of the second millennium since leaving Earth, the *Centauri Princess* was sailing the dark emptiness of that imaginary zone just over a trillion miles out, beyond which the Sun would cease to remain the most supreme source of light. That zone was of course known as the *'Ahad radius'*.

Sharuk Rashid's brick-like, tanned face appeared on ship television:-

'Our starship is about to officially enter the zone of permanent night, and will continue to sail in the darkness for the next forty five thousand years purely by the light of the stars in the surrounding cosmic night sky. We are approximately a trillion miles out from the Sun and our ancestor's home planet of Earth. From this point on, the Sun will no longer be the most dominant source of illumination in the sky exterior to the starship. We will be, quite literally, sailing by pure star light...'

This relay was being watched by five people sitting in

the lounge of a wooden-built house, located several miles away from the miniature world's main residential city of Utopia. The television was a state-of-the art, super-plasma screen, holographically projected device. It delivered the broadcasts in style; giving a 'virtual 3D' effect on all its pictures and sound. The folks back on Earth had done their utmost to provide the most up to date technology onboard this epic ark ship that was to carry the spirit of all that humanity ever stood for on that distant, blue-white globe.

'Big deal. The Sun never appeared a whole lot brighter than any other star every time I looked at it from the observation deck,' said Alcyone, a twenty one year old female ecosystem researcher (her name was pronounced "al-sai-own").

She enjoyed her wide ranging career, working in the starship's Environmental office. Keeping the oxygen/CO_2 balance right across the miniature ecosystem, was an important role. And doing something important for a job mattered to her a lot.

'I'm going out to get some air. Anyone care to join me for a walk?' She said, smiling thinly and dropped a hint toward a rather handsome young man sitting in the far corner.

He was called Joey. A twenty five year old astronautical engineer who, amongst his many other varied duties, presently supported the navigation team in the main control room, close to Utopia. He was also Alcyone's fiancé.

He followed her out. They walked along the quiet suburban street, a romantic sort of walk, conversing about the coming weekend and plans for them to go boating on the starship's one and only river.

It was a sunshiny kind of summer's day - or at least the *Centauri Princess'* equivalent of such a scene. Inside this artificially created world sailing between the stars, there was no sun in the sky of course. Powerful sun-simulating lights erected overhead onto transparent posts, towered above the tops of tall pine trees. Collectively, they threw down full spectrum sunlight across the starship's six hundred square kilometres of interior surface area. The overlapping cones of light rays coming down from those artificial 'suns', created an ambience which was virtually indistinguishable from that of natural sunshine experienced on Earth.

An eagle flew across the street, and it caught Alcyone's gaze. It perched itself high up on a tree branch, toward the deeper pine forest stretching out adjacent to the street.

Joey followed her gaze to take a look.

'She must be nesting up there,' he said.

Alcyone glanced further upwards into the sky, placing her right hand above her forehead to blot out distracting rays from a miniature sun nearby. She saw the other side of the starship's interior, curving around the sky past a darkish middle ground. Distant forests and small settlements looked misty, six miles overhead.

'Yes, I think so. But you know, she's a long way from the Wildlife Preserve over on the other side, and it's still too early for migration to have started,' she remarked, glancing back at him.

Joey had thick, styled dark hair and bluish eyes. He was fascinated by the night sky and the wonders of the vast universe that surrounded the lonely ark ship on its silent march towards eternity. He also had a habit of merging his scientific interests with philosophy. As they walked on, admiring the picturesque flora and fauna around them, he got philosophical.

'I wonder what it would be like if we ever get to meet E.T. one day.'

Alcyone glanced at him, looking puzzled.

'Excuse me?'

'Extraterrestrial intelligence. I read it in the historical archives of Earth. People once thought there had to be some form of life elsewhere in the universe other than on Earth. Since we're the first ones heading out into the cosmos, we may become the first to make contact.'

'I think we'll cross that bridge when we come to it Joey. Right now, I gotta get to Utopia before the stores close for the day. I'll see you tonight.'

Alcyone broke off the conversation and increased her pace to a brisk jog toward the mono rail station, seen coming up ahead of them at the end of the street.

'Last shuttle of the day. You wouldn't want to miss this one,' said the attendant at the station.

'Phew! Thought I almost did,' Alcyone said.

Inside the hi-tec shuttle train, she found a quiet compartment where a middle aged couple were sitting. The man glanced at her and smiled as a polite gesture of welcoming. She returned the smile.

The starship's primary means of transport to go from one location to another across the curved interior, was via a mono rail system. For the more financially well-off residents, there were small, fuel cell powered rovers, that looked much like cars on present day Earth. They offered complete independence and freedom of travel between Utopia and the broader countryside, going out beyond its environs. However, given the limited number of roads and the overall amount of surface area available across the miniature world, there was a restriction on only one such vehicle permitted to be owned per household. That arrangement worked perfectly well, since the total starship population had never exceeded the present figure of just three thousand, so far into the voyage.

Much of the six hundred square-kilometre interior surface area was densely forested by a mixture of largely evergreen and some deciduous trees. These produced all of the starship's oxygen, which was breathed in by people and animals, who in turn breathed out carbon dioxide and thus kept the biosphere in a self-sustaining, ecological cycle across the generations. Nitrogen in the miniature world's atmosphere was kept within Earthly proportions; its inert properties helped keep its share static over time. Fundamentally, here was perhaps the finest example of a world flourishing with life, that had the perfect order of natural harmony and equilibrium between all its various contributing elements. Its delicate design permitted little room for too much deforestation or over-urbanisation.

Seated by one of the large windows inside the mono rail train, Alcyone looked out towards the horizon in the distance, which showed the distinct curvature of the cylindrical interior of the *Centauri Princess*. Pine forests and lakes could be seen to extend all the way, as far as the eye could see, across the exotic landscape. The relief profile of this dreamlike world generally ranged from flat lowlands to gently rising hills, with some jagged rocky outcrops occasionally spiking up here and there to conjure up flash images of fairy tales set in the midst of castles in the mountains.

Joanna's was the most renowned store in western Utopia to be selling fashionable women's garments and other accessories. The dazzlingly lit, trendily laid out store bustled with crowds, who were wrapping up their purchases in earnest just as closing time was approaching.

Alcyone made somewhat of a rushed choice on buying a dress. Emerging from the fitting rooms more or less satisfied with her choice, she was pleasantly surprised to have spotted Caroline across over on the other side. They met up with kisses on cheeks and a hug, surprised not to have seen one another for about four weeks.

Caroline Polansky was twenty four, and had been a close friend of Alcyone's going back to their high school days. Although she had somewhat of a glamorous, sophisticated profile and an outgoing personality, Caroline was also caring in nature. With a tall, slender complexion and blue eyes and blonde hair, she had stunningly good looks, too.

'Hey, what's this I hear you've split with Sharuk, what actually happened? I thought the two of you were getting it together really well,' Alcyone said, with a surprised look.

'It was a little like that to begin with. I guess then things started to go wrong,' Caroline said.

Alcyone could sense this was no amicable break up. She tried to lighten things up.

'Are you sure? There's a lot of great looking guys at the Med you know, that can be hard to resist. Hey, somebody's been fooling around…' She teased, referring to the ship's Medical Facility building at the heart of Utopia, where Caroline worked.

'Nope, nothing like that I'm afraid !' Caroline giggled, as they hurried over to join the rapidly advancing queue at the automated payments till.

'So what else is new?' Alcyone prompted.

'I don't know quite how to put this, but I had this really weird dream the other night. It was weird.'

'Weird, as in *weird*?' Alcyone said, quizzically.

'I guess.' Caroline seemed reluctant to elaborate further. 'How about you?' She asked.

'Well not exactly, although I've heard it mentioned by a few people at my work place. Something about clouds of darkness coming from space.'

'Oh it's a little weirder than that, but never mind.' Caroline had plenty of brighter things to think about on this beautiful afternoon.

The queue moved along and it was Alcyone's turn to pay for her dress, lipstick and other odds and ends she had picked up in the store. The barcode reader automatically scanned the items in her hand. She pointed her wristcom at a device on the automated checkout. It acknowledged the transaction with a tuneful bleep and a 'Thank you for your custom. Please call again soon,' message on its display.

The 'wristcom' was an all-embracing technology bracelet which everyone wore as part of their standard attire, that served as both a fashion accessory and equally a multi-function device for audio/video telecoms, electronic payments and time keeping, amongst countless other features. An electronic payment system, utilising a common currency called 'E.M.'—short for 'exchange medium'—had been in use throughout their world ever since its departure from Earth. The E.M. units were electronically kept on deposit in a person's bank account, which was centrally maintained by the starship's banking facility in Utopia; but equally, the account was made remotely accessible via the wristcom bracelets, which periodically updated the central bank with all recorded debits and credits.

The starship's central computer was referred to as 'CPC' by everyone - short for *Centauri Princess Central Intelligence*. It managed the financial system operating across their miniature world, much like how the monetary system is managed by a central bank within a small state here on Earth today.

'Hey why don't we go see a movie this coming Saturday night? There's a highly renowned comedy show on at the multi screen,' Caroline said cheerily.

'I'd love to. But we're going on a river boat cruise along Eridanus by day and having a quiet night in at Joey's place.'

'Sounds like a lot of fun in store for you guys.'

'I hope so.'

Alcyone looked out onto the street, where the miniature suns threw a late afternoon peach orange glow across the scene. 'We're in for a nice evening. Let's go for a pizza at Magellan's after this, what do you say?' She suggested.

'Okay let's invite Alissa too, she's into pizzas.'

Caroline called Alissa, who was equally an acquaintance of Alcyone's, on her wristcom as they stepped out of Joanna's fashion store. She invited Alissa to meet up at Magellan's pizza restaurant in about half an hour.

Just then, Sharuk drove up in his blue, open top rover. He had rather affectionately named his vehicle 'Corvette', after the vintage Earth vehicle of the twentieth century by the same name. He parked up in front of Joanna's, having spotted Alcyone and Caroline on the sidewalk.

'I just want us to talk,' he called out to Caroline.

She shrugged, giving him a glaring look.

'I'll wait here,' prompted Alcyone.

Caroline hesitantly wandered over to his rover, and looked down at him.

'What the heck do you want to talk about?'

He took off his black sunglasses. 'Us. I thought you might want to,' he said, quietly.

She looked him in the eye. 'It's over Sharuk. I thought we'd been through this several times before. You found someone more to your liking and I just want to get on with my life, so just leave me alone. You got that?'

'I still want us to be friends and I've also got some guilty feelings about all of this, okay?' Sharuk tried his best to sound apologetic.

'Guilty feelings, huh? You could have fooled me. Just leave me alone,' she said sternly, and then turned away to rejoin Alcyone. They walked on.

'I was meaning to tell you this for a while, I've been hearing rumours that this guy seemingly has a track record of dumping people after short relationships. How could that creep do this to you?' Alcyone said sympathetically.

'How many guys does it take to find the *true* one? Thanks Als, I'll get over it.' Caroline felt stronger with the moral support from her friend.

They wandered off towards Magellan's pizza restaurant a few blocks away on the west side of central Utopia.

'East' and 'west' on the *Centauri Princess* were defined as, respectively, pointing toward the front and rear of the starship's nine mile-long, cylindrical interior. 'North' and 'south' were non-existent terms inside this miniature world; instead, one would simply refer to the 'Lower' or 'Upper' province where a particular landmark or feature was located. The Lower and Upper provinces were a broadly fifty-fifty split of the starship's six mile-wide biosphere cylinder, with the dividing line running along the central spin axis of the giant starship. For specific location coordinates, the wristcom worn by each individual kept grid references that pinpointed exact locations which updated in real time, as people roamed around the interior.

The *Centauri Princess'* central governing body was the Mission Management Committee (MMC). It consisted of a panel of a hundred people, who were in charge of separate functions such as medical, navigation, engineering, mining, ecology, environmental, and so on. The MMC was headed by a starship president, who had the ultimate, final decision-making powers concerning mission management and strategy.

Amongst its wide ranging responsibilities, the MMC placed extremely high emphasis on good schooling for young children, as this was naturally one of the fundamental pillars for ensuring a stable societal structure in this multi-generational voyage. Starting from an early age, through school, college and university, children were brought up in a culture of understanding and mutual respect for one another, and the communities were kept very cohesive as a result of knowing their complete isolation. People went through life, fully aware of the vulnerabilities if they rocked the boat in the middle of nowhere…thousands of years and trillions of miles away from any other world. In order to deliver the right kind of education, teachers were selected and trained for their posts through strict personality and calibre tests; in particular, they needed to have a pretty high philanthropic bias and adhere to good moral standards.

Nikolaus Zakarov, forty years old and a descendant from the Russian Federation by Earth origins, was one person who met all of those standards. He was a successful man in just about every possible way. A character of handsome good looks and stature, he had a successful career behind him spanning multiple roles, with sufficient wealth accumulated to be able to own a suburban town house of renowned grandeur. A few women had weaved their way in and out of his life over the years, but not even one of his relationships lasted into anything permanent enough for him to tie that knot or even settle into any long term commitments. His wide ranging and distinguished career, supplemented by a multitude of spare time interests, mostly took priority. Although his main background was in electrical engineering and taking command of the starship's extravehicular operations, Zakarov also filled in technical roles in the Navigation and Control Complex in Utopia. He was also a part-time science teacher at the Lower Province's Redwood Junior School.

On this occasion, he was coming to the end of a lecture on the basics of spaceflight. He sat at the front of the extensive classroom, with a large electronic screen behind him serving as an old-style 'blackboard', used for interactive tuition in conjunction with plasma screen terminals mounted on each child's desk.

'Finally, if we take a look at this animation here, we see that Newton's third law is very much at work in whizzing our super-speed rocket through space. The amount of forward thrust delivered to the rocket is proportional to the force with which the exhaust gases are ejected out from the back,' he said in a moderately deep voice.

'And that folks, just about concludes our lesson for today. Now, does anyone have any questions for me?'

Alcyone's niece, who was eight years old and sitting in a far corner of the classroom, raised her hand.

'Yes Irene, fire away.'

'Are we alone in the universe?' Asked the little girl. Her question was clearly a little off-topic and she looked slightly confused.

'That's a very good question. The short answer is most probably not. See, we are here—' he pointed to the star-studded screen behind him showing a view of the

Centauri Princess in space, '—in our own little world aboard this ship, but all around us, as far as the eye can see, there are billions upon billions of stars and distant galaxies. Circling around many of these stars there are much larger worlds than the one we're in, called 'planets'. We believe a large number of them have life and some of them even have people, just like us, living on them. We ourselves have left behind our ancestors on a planet called Earth, right about here.'

He pointed to a yellowish speck of light on the screen, which was of course our own distant Sun, shining like an exceptionally brilliant star in the inky black skies exterior to the starship.

'Are there any more questions?' Asked the teacher. There was only silence. 'Okay. Class dismissed, see you all next week. Mind how you go now.'

The children rushed off to board the school bus waiting outside on the main road, that ran through the Lower Province's educational complex.

Zakarov gathered the assignment papers handed to him by each pupil as they had left the classroom, neatly stacking them into a briefcase for later marking over the weekend. Although, by far, the bulk of all information exchange on the ship was through electronic means, the written word on paper never lost its shine across the generations. The huge abundance of trees growing in the woodlands across the interior provided an endless supply of recyclable, quality writing paper. And so the old Earth traditions of textbooks and writing in ink remained with the ongoing generations.

Zakarov left the school building via its long porch,

extending out to the front and drove home in his open top rover, which he had rather affectionately nicknamed 'Betty'. It was common practice for people to name their fuel cell powered vehicles after someone or something personal to them. Zakarov had once owned a Labrador retriever by the same name, but tragically that dog had to be put down following a near fatal accident involving a malfunctioned robot that had lost its fly-around orientation, crashing into Betty with a devastating blow.

He turned into the gravel driveway of his luxury built town house of a few stories high, set in the midst of beautiful pine forests a couple of miles west of Utopia. The place towered before him like a castle set against the lush green, scenic backdrop. As he went inside, a wooden staircase stared at him from the end of the hall way, that led up to the upper floors. The interior design perfectly suited his elegant tastes. Modern furniture mixed with antiques; walls laced with exquisite artwork, that was obscured by the occasional painting hanging here and there. They looked dated, and were from a few of the *Centauri Princess'* more noted artists of bygone eras.

Winding down from a hectic day at work, he relaxed on the sofa in the ground floor lounge, having grabbed some freshly squeezed grapefruit juice from the fridge. He used his wristcom as a remote control device to put on one of his all-time favourite classical music tracks on the interactive screen, that was embedded into the lounge's far side wall.

The 'screen' was a universal feature in all the homes and commercial buildings across the interior. In addition to being wirelessly networked to the central computer,

CPC, it incorporated a whole range of features, including entertainment services from music, TV, video, radio through to serving as a communication device that supplemented the personal wristcoms.

As he sat back, appreciating the drink and tuneful melody filling the room, his wristcom pulsed with a message.

'Unc it's Caroline. I'll be over in about ten minutes.'

'Okay, see you shortly,' he said, as her image faded from the tiny screen of the metallic wristcom.

Caroline Polansky regarded her uncle, Zakarov as a fatherly figure in whom she could often confide for sharing personal ups and downs in life. Yesterday, she had left him a message saying there was something she wanted to talk about and would be around to see him.

Moments later, both uncle and niece were in the lounge of his town house. She looked a bit down in contrast to her usual cheery self, as she poured some coffee from a machine nearby.

Zakarov drank juice from the glass in his right hand. He had a small hint of her reasons for coming over.

'This is about you and Sharuk, right? I hope the two of you've managed to patch things up since I last saw you.'

Caroline was visibly depressed, as she walked over and took her seat on the sofa opposite him.

'It's over.'

'I'm really sorry to hear this What the hell has he been up to now, that good for nothing…so and so!?' Zakarov said, angrily.

'It's a long story.'

Caroline took some time to explain in detail how things had gone down hill over the past few weeks. Not being able to judge her ex's character well enough early on in the relationship, left her feeling cheated and totally used.

Eventually, brushing aside her own affairs, she wanted to hear his side of things.

'How's work for you, Unc?'

Zakarov gulped down the remaining drink. He placed the empty glass on the table with a slight thump.

'Hectic. There's been a major malfunction of electrostatic cloud stimulation high up over the farming complex. They've not been getting any rains for the past few weeks, and it's looking bad for the rice crops.' Zakarov explained his next engineering assignment.

'Sounds urgent.'

'I got to go and do a few repairs on one of the weatherbots—first thing tomorrow morning, in fact.'

The folks who managed the *Centauri Princess'* farming complex did so with one overriding goal: simply to provide the communities with a continuous supply of quality foods that met the varied dietary requirements across the ongoing generations.

The distinctive perimeter wall of the complex, constructed from a titanium alloy that glowed with a silvery shine, enclosed a vast area of nearly five square miles of domes and open-field rice plantations. The metallic astroculture domes housed the more exotic species of fruits and vegetables that required indoor cultivation. They also contained specialised compartments for poultry and cattle rearing. At this moment, the malfunction of one of the twenty odd weatherbots operating at high altitude along the sky length of the starship's interior, threatened the rice crops growing in the large, open fields across the complex.

A 'weatherbot' was simply an unmanned air vehicle that floated roughly three miles above the starship's interior, which generated an electrostatic charge that helped stimulate the high altitude clouds into releasing their water vapour content as rainfall.

As he drove across the farming complex in his rover, Zakarov scanned the gently curving plains going into the distance. Newly planted rice crops made the paddy fields appear yellowish-green in colour. The yellowish part of the look was a symptom of lack of rains; from previous visits to the complex and also from general knowledge, Zakarov was well aware that newly planted rice always had a greenish shine—if it were flourishing.

The odour of decaying marsh vegetation, mostly water hyacinths and low growing reeds from the paddy fields, mingled with cow and horse dung. They gave a farmland smell to the breezy, dry air.

Up ahead, half galloping toward his rover on horseback, he recognised a familiar face. She slowed the horse to a gentle walk on noticing him. He eased back the speed of his semi-autonomous, silvery-grey metallic vehicle.

'Zakarov dear, what brings you to us?' Said the rider, as she passed by along the farming complex's main road.

'Well, if it isn't the young Karyn Colaco. Howdy ma'am. I'm going to put a stop to the dry season and try and bring you folks some torrential showers around here,' Zakarov said.

'Well, be sure to drop by for some warm coffee and a chat after you finish the job.'

'I'll try.'

Karyn waved back at him, holding up her hand as the silver horse began to speed up again toward a gallop.

Zakarov reached the main hub of the farming complex. He parked Betty outside the building that housed the Control Centre, and went inside. Six feet in height and with a solid build, he walked like a panther along the corridor, towards the reception suite.

'Hello. I'm Nikolaus Zakarov, here to see to the malfunctioned weatherbot,' he said to the fair haired, male receptionist.

'Good to see you sir. We have been expecting you. Please go right through, the tech lab is over to your left along the corridor.'

Zakarov sat in front of the video console and browsed the screen showing repairbots that had the status of being vacant and available in the neighbourhood at this particular moment in time. Number 56 was flashing on the bluish monitor screen as the closest and immediately ready for commanding. He typed in a message in technical language, instructing the flight-capable repairbot to go up to the three mile high, hovering weatherbot that needed fixing.

A 'repairbot' was originally a generic name given to a fleet of highly capable, semi-autonomous intelligent machines that could be commanded to carry out essential maintenance and repair tasks around the vast ship. Nowadays of course, repairbots did a lot more than simply repair things; the range of applications to which they lent their services was enormous. Everything, from sampling air temperatures at high altitude to carrying out maintenance of the lighting system, replacing the sun-simulating light bulbs by flying up to them when they burned out, to helping the elderly and the infirm starship residents with their day to day shopping and grocery needs…the task list could go on, almost forever. Name a manual, labour intensive job and a repairbot could do it. They were broadly divided into two categories: industrial and domestic. The latter variety were allocated to families and homes, serving the roles of personal assistants and pet robots around the house.

Of course repairbots themselves needed servicing by humans from time to time, although typically, their inter-service schedules ran into decades. The Manufacturing & Robotics Facilities, based in the *Princess'* Lower Province, were responsible for keeping the repairbot fleet fully operational at all times.

Having reached its three mile high target, Number 56 relayed back a diagnostics report to the tech lab where Zakarov was sitting in front of the command console. It showed the weatherbot was simply out of batteries for powering its electrostatic lightning amplifier. Zakarov commanded a replacement of the fifty year life span batteries with spares carried onboard within the repairbot's tool box. Number 56 humbly obeyed, using its finely articulated robotic arms it removed the sealed battery cover on the weatherbot, took out the dead batteries, and revitalised the unit with a fresh power supply.

A few minutes later, having safely distanced itself by propelling away from the weatherbot, Number 56 performed a test on the restored unit. It sparked a hundred million volt-charged lightning flash, that momentarily lit up the dark skies high above the farming complex. A sky-busting rumble of thunder was then heard, which shook the tech lab where Zakarov was working. Rainfall was witnessed shortly afterwards across the farming complex, and from where he was sitting, Zakarov could see the gentle downpour in front of him through the tech lab's window. The rain drops never fell vertically down; they descended from the sky following a more gentler, curved glide path under the 'weird' gravity conditions of this exotic world. At last, the rice fields were awash with new rains. Almost as he watched, they were resuming their healthy, emerald green shine across the curved landscape.

Saturday afternoon

Eridanus flowed from one edge of Utopia, meandering all the way around the cylindrical ship, straddling both its Lower and Upper provinces, and back to the other end of the city. Almost everyone at some point or other took boating breaks along its length. This would often be on a day's outing as a vacation-like treat. Sometimes, it might be quite simply to refresh one's self from all the work related city stress experienced in the starship's day to day operations.

The river was fairly shallow in depth, about two hundred feet across at its widest points and it had an ever so gently flowing current. Its banks gradually sloped down from the surrounding landscape, and the water's edges were naturally decorated by exotic looking reeds and pink flowering water lilies, growing freely near the banks on both sides. An occasional heron could be seen catching fish from Eridanus' turquoise-tinged waters, in almost any season around the year.

The present season in the *Centauri Princess'* miniature world was approaching early summer (equivalent to early June in the northern temperate latitudes of Earth), simulated by CPC with appropriate lighting and temperature adjustments. Hence, there was a profusion of brightly coloured flowers swaying in the gentle summer breeze across the marsh-like banks of Eridanus. At this instant, the display was made even more striking by the late afternoon sunshine simulation across the interior, throwing a yellowish light onto the landscape.

Here on Earth, the position of the sun in the sky will vary according to the time of day, the point along the seasonal cycle of the year that you happen to be in and your geographic latitude. All of these factors dictate the inclination with which the sun's rays strike the landscape and the overall amount of light and heat that's generated. They create an ever changing atmosphere and ambience that gives one a sense of time and place reference that is completely natural and independently appreciated by our senses without the need to refer to a wrist watch or look at a calendar.

Of course inside this exotic world of the *Centauri Princess*, where miniature suns were positionally fixed on tops of their hundred metre-high, transparent pedestals and from where they beamed down onto the landscape around you, there could be no such comparisons to Earth when it came to gauging time reference purely by one's senses. However, CPC had its own inbuilt programming to control the level of lighting in order to maintain virtually Earth-like seasonal and diurnal sunshine profiles across the ship.

The level of lighting was adjusted according to a model that was exactly matched to conditions at one specific location on the Earth's surface. It just so happened that the sunshine profile in the ship mirrored exactly that experienced by a person who was living on the latitude line marked by the *49th parallel* on Earth. This was simply because the technology plant where the starship's diurnal/seasonal cycle control was designed and manufactured, prior to launch, happened to have been sited half way between Seattle and Vancouver in North America.

The team behind its design had simply found it to be practical to mirror that site's seasonal profile inside the ship. It worked well since the mission's overall goal was to simulate a definite 'four seasons' profile, which would have been lacking had the seasonal variations been modelled on a more tropical locale like Orlando, Florida, where a sister technology plant was sited in the *Centauri Princess* construction programme.

The winter season across the starship interior thus provided just eight hours of daylight around the time of the winter solstice, which doubled to sixteen hours toward the peak day lengths in early summer, as at present. The extreme seasonal swings in temperatures experienced along the *49th parallel* on Earth, however, were never matched across the interior of the ship, simply because the plants and animals had been acclimatised more toward subtropical conditions. Thus, the *Centauri Princess'* residents never encountered snowfall, for example, within their idyllic world.

Alcyone had been looking forward to a river boat excursion for several weeks, since first booking the venue on the suggestion of a friend at work. Joey met her at the boating harbour at four o'clock sharp, as prearranged, and they started the ride from the western edge of Utopia. The boat's small engine made a soft, purring sound as Joey slotted in a pre-programmed cartridge into its control console.

As with land vehicles like rovers and the mono rail train, the engine of the boat was powered by fuel cells; a clean energy solution operated throughout the ship in order to keep its interior clean. As a starship-wide rule, no chemical fuels were ever burnt in any activity that could lead to pollution. The biosphere and ecosystem were thus well preserved and kept in an idyllic, tip-top shape over the myriad of ongoing generations.

Joey, often quite absent minded about such things, felt aware of something unusual about Alcyone's appearance on this excursion. After eyeing her over and pondering for a bit, he figured out what it was.

'Love your new dress. It seems to go really well with your gorgeous looking, greenish eyes,' he remarked romantically.

My god, he noticed. Wow! Alcyone thought.

'I'm glad you like it. Cost me a thousand E-Ms at Joanna's last week. Incidentally that was when I also bumped into Caroline in the store.'

'Miss Centauri Princess herself? Haven't seen her around for a while,' he said teasingly, 'boy, that girl is such a hottie!'

'Jo-eeyy!' yelled Alcyone.

'Sor-ry.' He gave her a coy look. 'Hey, she may be cute but you *know* you're the girl of my dreams, right?'

She looked at him and smiled, feeling somewhat flattered.

Alcyone stood at the front of the boat, admiring the picturesque scene looking along the length of the river straight ahead. It meandered its way into the distance, gradually curving upward towards the 'sky', as it followed the cylindrical profile of the *Centauri Princess'* interior. Its waters surrounding the small motor boat had a distinctly turquoise tinge, which reflected occasional clouds that slowly drifted across the dark sky, overhead. Swarms of large, blue-green winged dragon flies hovered above the subtropical waters, adding their specially adapted colours to the picturesque splendour.

Whilst she admired the scenic views, Joey was admiring her sultry looks. With her slender figure, dark brown hair tied loosely back into a pony tail and the new dress enhancing her shapely outline, he felt captivated by the very essence of her.

He reached down and produced a bottle of premium quality, exotic juice from a chiller in the boat's picnic compartment. He stood up again, and took a swig of the synthesised, coconut flavoured drink.

'Well, here we are, sailing the great river of Eridanus,' he said in a captain's tone.

'Damn lucky to have found a free boating slot with all

the demand for it this season,' she said, turning around to face him. 'Ah, pina colada. My favourite!'

She reached for the alcohol-free drink. He moved it out of her reach.

'Say please.'

'Joey, just give me the damn bottle…'

The boat was lightly rocked in the pushing and shoving.

Out of the picnic compartment, he drew out a second bottle of the popular drink and offered it to her. They sat back on the leisurely cruise, soaking in the afternoon sunshine and sipping exotic juice.

'I wonder why it's called Eridanus. I mean why not simply 'The River' or something like that, as it's the only one we've got?' Alcyone asked, pausing between two swigs.

'You know, for someone who's named after the brightest star in the Pleiades, you really don't know much about the night sky do you? Eridanus is a long, sprawling river constellation shining in the cosmic night sky around the ship, and they named this river after that,' Joey said, knowledgeably.

'So they did. And the Pleiades are a cluster of sapphire blue, young stars commonly known as the *Seven Sisters*, and I was named after one of them.'

'Unless I'm missing something here, you haven't got seven sisters. So how come your mom and dad named you after one of the Pleiades?'

She giggled.

'Seven?! Gosh, no. Having just one sister is more than enough, if you've got the right one. As for 'Alcyone', well my daddy chose to call me that. I guess he just wanted to give me a pretty name, 'cos he loved me a lot.'

'Daddy's girl, huh?'

She lay back onto a cushion, set deeply within the central deck of the boat. He joined her, and they engaged in a romantic conversation. As her eyes met his, Alcyone felt the most wonderful surge of passion sweep through her. Sensing her needs, as if it were the most natural thing in the world to do, he kissed her...

From a lying down position on this calmly moving river boat, looking directly overhead at the dark sky, they saw an aerial view of Utopia across to the starship's opposite side. The scene resembled a view looking down from a jumbo jet here on Earth, that was climbing toward a thirty seven thousand feet cruising altitude above a city, shortly after take-off. Only here, that aerial view was inverted, and placed in the 'sky' of this exotic world. The vast array of Utopia's shingle roofed buildings could be seen glinting six miles overhead, with Eridanus itself meandering like a snake through the centre of the idyllic city.

Towards the end of their excursion, the starship's evening had arrived with the automated lighting system gradually dimming to simulate a sunset across the interior.

On Earth, at dusk when the sun gradually begins to set, its rays are seen to strike the landscape from a more oblique angle with the longer wavelengths in the orange and red end of the spectrum having more strength to penetrate through a thicker layer of the atmosphere. Thus all objects in the surrounding landscape are seen to glow in an orangish hue. These same sunset colours were presently mirrored in the glow cast across the forested landscape throughout the *Centauri Princess*, where subtle variations in the colour and intensity of its lighting system were gradually altered through precision control of the miniature suns, by CPC.

By the time they docked the motor boat at the other end of Utopia and made it to Joey's place, it was almost nightfall and the last illumination of day was seen to leak away into the engulfing darkness. A light sprinkle of localised rain began to drench the grounds and green shrubbery surrounding Joey's house, just as they rushed indoors at the start of an evening thunder storm.

The weather phenomena inside the *Centauri Princess* was expected to be rather exotic and often unpredictable, due to the constant change in direction of gravity vectors from the ship's artificial gravity spin.

Later in the evening, Alcyone cooked a meal for herself and Joey. After supper, they finally retired to bed, having flicked through the television channels and finding nothing of particular interest.

Following a mild version of the nightmare syndrome she experienced the previous night, Alcyone hoped for more pleasant sleep tonight. Strangely enough, Joey had not yet experienced any bad dreams as such, and he was snoring away peacefully soon after they'd kissed goodnight. More than likely exhausted from their long river boat excursion earlier in the day, she thought.

4. Angels from the darkness

On this occasion, Alcyone's nightmare began at the dead of night, around two thirty in the small hours when the streets of Utopia outside had fallen into a deathly silence. The lamps just beyond the front garden's perimeter fence had been dimmed to a tiny, candle-like glow by CPC.

As the nightmare crawled into the sleeping consciousness of her mind (rather like a blanket of fog rolling in from the oceans over a coastal town on Earth), Alcyone found herself standing on the starship's observation deck all by herself. She was staring through its large window out into black space. She did not know for what purpose she was there nor how she got to be there in the first place, as she had hardly been one for stargazing. Somehow, she was just *there* staring out into the black void filled with tiny pin pricks of light, scattered across the cosmic night.

As the ship turned in its artificial gravity spin, taking

some two and a half minutes to complete one full rotation, the stars drifted across the field of view. They took some ten to twelve seconds to gently glide across the rectangular window of the observation deck. Alcyone noticed how the currents of warm air rising from the deck's outlet vents close to her feet, caused the brighter stars to twinkle in an ever pleasant colourful display, that was reminiscent of glittering gemstones in a jewellery store.

But then she noticed something rather odd...as if a cloud of engulfing darkness was somehow beginning to blot out some of the stars, gradually cutting out their light from view. The fainter stars were the first to vanish, as if some phantom catastrophe of immeasurable proportions was wiping out a huge corner of the great Milky Way galaxy stretching out in front of her. On a more closer glance, she noticed there was something rather odd about this cloud of evolving darkness: it did not appear to be of uniform opacity throughout. Rather, it seemed to be condensing into five distinct blotches, each one taking on a complex shape...

In the depths of her sleep Alcyone stirred, as her eyes continued to twitch in the deepening nightmare. With the slowly passing seconds, in her mind's eye she could see the cloud of engulfing darkness materialise into five different entities. She witnessed each one gradually take on the shape of a winged, wolf-like creature. The scene was now more than a mere silhouette cast against the backdrop of the starry sky, with facial features softly materialising on the distant beasts. On each entity, the head appeared more distinct and less camouflaged than the wings, with deeply set, glowing red eyes, a muzzle with a snout, white teeth and a pair of ferocious-looking fangs. Compared to wolves, however, the faces of the beasts materialising here were much thinner; squeezed horizontally and somewhat stretched vertically, they looked utterly demonic. The illusive creatures appeared to be slowly flapping their wings as they drifted in from the depths of space, as if they were flying through air. They gradually edged closer toward the window, from where Alcyone watched in horror.

Heavily camouflaged and merged against the backdrop of the cosmic night, they seemed to be flying in a roughly even formation. The central creature in the pack led the other four, flanked in pairs to its either side. Suddenly, they appeared to leap forward in their ghostly glide- a menacing advance- as if the glazed window of the ship's observation deck were of no consequence to them.

Alcyone screamed in her nightmare. She felt momentarily disoriented; no sound would come from her vocal chords, as if her surreal state of existence had somehow disabled her normal bodily functions. She found herself frozen with horror and wanted to run to escape the advancing evil, but her feet seemed to be glued to the concrete floor where she stood helpless. She gasped out in terror, and tried to tear herself away from the apparition. At last, she was physically released from the grip of fear. Turning away from the advancing beasts, she began a frantic run along the corridor stretching out in front of her. The observation deck's elevator beckoned, holding its doors wide open about a hundred feet away.

She threw herself into the small cubicle of the elevator. Now there seemed to be yet another problem in this surreal state of her present existence: the automated doors simply would not close. Gripped in panic, Alcyone tried to find her voice. She commanded 'Close doors!' into the microphone of the voice-operated control box, but once again no sound would come from her throat. She fumbled for the emergency backup button nearby, and hit it with the palm of her right hand just in time to get the doors drawing toward a close.

To her even more shock and horror, a split-second before the two sliding doors met up to a fully sealed close, the archangel of the advancing beasts managed to squeeze its ferocious muzzle through into the elevator. Its eyes glowed an intense red, as it snarled fiercely, exposing its razor-sharp teeth and fangs. The phantom beast vented a cloud of mist from its nostrils that filled the small cubicle with an evil stench...

Alcyone screamed as loud as she could. At last she found herself awake in bed with a cold sweat, gasping for breath next to Joey. He grabbed her by the shoulders and tried to calm her down, as she continued to shudder. He turned up the dimmer switch for the bedroom light.

'We'll go and see a psychoanalyst first thing Monday morning,' he said, feeling powerless to be able to do anything more.

'What the heck is wrong with me! That's the second night in a row, and I'm getting sick and tired of this.'

She jumped out of bed and prepared herself a hot chocolate drink from a machine nearby, just outside the bedroom.

'This is getting out of hand Joey. I lose concentration during the day, and it affects my job.'

Next day, on a quiet Sunday morning, Alcyone was up bright and early although Joey was much more restful, having a bit of a lie in. She had a bite to eat for breakfast consisting of a slice of toast with jam and some tea. For her, Sundays were always days dedicated to pure leisure, be it going to visit a friend, listening to music or going for a stroll in the countryside. On this day, she decided to go for a quiet walk, to reflect generally on life and everything else. Alcyone was like that. Always the more quiet and reflective one out of her and her elder sister, Rujina. With memories of traumatic nightmares from the night before still vivid in her mind, she needed a bit of space to herself.

'Where are you going?' asked Joey, half a wake in bed and rubbing his eyes.

'Just a short walk to Caroline's place. I'll be back by lunch time, or just after.'

'Sure you feeling okay after last night?' He sounded concerned.

'I'll be fine.'

She kissed him lightly, and left the house by the back door.

Caroline lived on the outskirts of Utopia, across the famous *diamond bridge* over Eridanus river in a suburban street on the other side of town. Her street was called Inertia Drive, as if to remind folks of the science-driven design of this miniature world.

Since the start of her walk, now approaching mid-morning, Alcyone noticed how quiet the street looked all around, with rows of houses on both sides looking silent. This half of Utopia being a predominantly Christian sector meant everyone's still indoors, observing the Sunday, 'day of rest' thing, she realised.

Virtually all of the houses on the ship were built from wood, and the majority of them looked awfully similar to homes in the deep southern states of America, in the twenty first century. That same greyish, painted look on the outside, complete with verandas at the front and trees growing in the front yard, along the sides and at the back. The *Centauri Princess'* folk had to maintain an ecologically friendly culture in all that they did, since they were totally dependent on preserving their plants, animals and forests to safeguard their own survival across the ongoing generations. Hence, once trees were felled from the forests, they would be put through an effective recycling process by using the timber for production of paper, household furniture and of course, in building new homes.

Alcyone passed the local bakers store on the corner of the junction between Emerald Crescent and Lakeview Road. She waved hello to Mr. Schlesinger through the window, who waved back at her with a smile. The brown haired man inside was always kind natured and reminded Alcyone of her father. The same features, the same build, even the clothes he wore and the friendly mannerisms with which he would serve his customers, all made her feel very nostalgic about the father that she had once loved.

She remembered that fateful day just over eleven years ago, when disaster had struck the space shuttle that both her parents were riding in during a routine fly around of the *Centauri Princess*. Somehow, that thirty minute leisurely flight happened to coincide with the ship passing through a fatal stream of interstellar dust particles. Each speck within the cloud measured some zero point three microns in diameter - a touch beyond the maximum permitted by the shuttle craft's ultra strong outer shielding. As a result, the high speed bombardment shattered cockpit windows without warning and caused them to disintegrate, killing all five people on board.

What was still a slight mystery was how the ship sensors never detected the upcoming debris cloud in front, although it was quite plausible that the expanse of the cloud was too insignificant for successful detection in time, in order to avert the disaster. As if it were of some consolation, there was a crucial element of luck in this incident. After the debris impact, the shuttle's autopilot had miraculously stayed intact, and managed to return the corpses to the shuttle landing bay area inside the starship, for a respectable burial.

Today being a Sunday and her having the vivid memories of her parents that she did, Alcyone now decided she would pay a visit to the cemetery and crematorium instead of going to Caroline's. The graveyard was located in the Lower Province, close to the Great Front Wall of the ship's cylindrical biosphere, nearly four miles from Utopia. Rather a long way to go for a quiet Sunday morning leisurely walk, she knew. But Alcyone felt decisive enough. She was driven by a sense of yearning, and just felt she had to pay her respects.

Joey got up late and after taking a quick shower, he went through the directory of starship services on the interactive screen. He was anxious to find someone who had some know-how on dreams, nightmares and alternative means of sleep therapy. CPC brought up a list of just three possible choices that matched the search criteria.

'Option one,' Joey said to the voice interactive screen, taking up the most highly recommended choice.

'Presto!' he exclaimed when the screen flashed up the details of a Karim Yurchenko, listed as a professional mystic, medium and dream therapist. Joey vaguely recognised the name as belonging to a character he had once come across at a Halloween party. The detailed description of his services showed Yurchenko lived all by himself near the edge of the Black Forest, close to the educational complex in the Lower Province. Fortunately, the mono rail route in its circumnavigating path around the ship, happened to run between the Black Forest and the educational complex, so Joey headed for the shuttle train at Utopia Central.

The approach path to the cemetery was gravelled and flanked by rose bushes on either side. A rusty, corrugated iron fence marked out its perimeter and ran all the way around, weaving its way through the groves of pine trees towering high above in the adjacent forest. Puddles of fresh rain water could be seen stretching along the path, going all the way into the graveyard. Alcyone took a deep breath of the post-thunder storm air, admiring the sweet fragrance from brightly coloured tea roses waving in the breeze nearby. As she reached the wide open gates, she paused to briefly scan the myriad of headstones littered across the grounds ahead of her.

The starship's internal giant Great Front Wall ran adjacent to the cemetery, a quarter of a mile beyond its eastern edge, on the other side of Eridanus river. The two circular ends of the cylindrical interior, one on either end, were grey in colour and never out of sight no matter from where one looked in their direction. Presently, Alcyone saw the six mile-high Great Front Wall towering over the cemetery as a grey, metallic backdrop. It looked like a perfectly smooth, vertical cliff face cut into the side of some fantasy world's mountain range. Only here, its expanse stretched from the ground going up all the way to the zenith (overhead) point - few fantasy worlds thus far created ever had such a landmark stretching between heaven and earth.

The cemetery grounds were always kept in partial darkness, so that even at the present local time close to midday, its illumination appeared significantly dimmer compared to the rest of the interior. This was in accord with a popular belief amongst the communities that the resting place of the dead ought to be given a more serene, shaded ambience, irrespective of what went on elsewhere throughout the starship. The place thus always had a permanently eerie look about it.

By religious background, Alcyone was brought up as a Christian from an early age, although her faith was never particularly strong in the religious sense. Later on in life, after meeting Joey, she had persuaded herself to convert to his own faith as a Muslim. The largely benign temperament of Utopian society at present, permitted such free thinking, free willing transfers between cultures and religions without let or hindrance.

Alcyone reached the two distinctively tall, adjacent

headstones that marked out her parents' graves. She stood there silently on the gravel path, reading the message inscribed on the pinkish-tinged, granite plaque that was common to both grave stones.

"Here rest in peace Mr and Mrs Cremona, who perished in the great disaster that struck the ill-fated EVA flight of March 12th, 4264 A.D...."

Alcyone was suddenly overcome by a deep sense of sadness that she had seldom felt before. In fact, she recalled, never. At least not since the early years that followed her parents' pass away. As was customary in Islamic faith, she wanted to say a little prayer that Joey had taught her several months ago. Alcyone just realised she had forgotten its intricate, Arabic verses.

Yurchenko's house was about five minutes walk from the mono rail station where Joey got dropped off, close to Redwood Junior School in the Lower Province. There was a small signpost nailed onto a nearby tree that briefly indicated Yurchenko's services, with its arrow pointing towards an opening into the dense forest.

Joey took the trail route cut through dense under growth leading into the Black Forest. He passed a butterfly bush that was currently in bloom, and noticed the swarms of exotic insects that had gathered on its amethyst-tinged flowers. They were attracted by the sweetly scented pollen. Overhead, he could hear the loud, hooting sound of what must have been a huge bird sitting high up on one of the conifer branches. As he passed underneath, alerted by his presence the creature took to flight upwards into the sky, flapping its large wings audibly. Joey realised at once he was right in thinking it could only have been a moiur ("moy-oor").

Moiurs were a variety of specially bred birds that were vaguely a cross between a peacock and a pheasant here on present day Earth. They were specially adapted for the voyage long before departure from Earth, specifically to take care of any overgrowth in swarms of flying insects inside the ship. Presently, although free to breed in the wild woodlands of the Black Forest, their numbers had to be monitored by the MMC and kept in balance with the delicate ecosystem harmony operating throughout the starship biosphere. For the starship's year to flow through in a natural cycle, with plants bearing blossoms and fruits with accurate seasonality like we are used to seeing in the here and now, pollinating insects such as bumble bees and wasps, along with certain other types of flies, needed to be carefully nurtured. Too many moiurs, and the insect population becomes inadequate; too few, and you end up with a plague. Thanks to the presence of these graceful birds, locust swarms—that can plague entire continents here on Earth—were never a problem in this enclosed mini-world, drifting in the endless interstellar oceans of space toward a near-infinitely far destination, still tens of thousands of years in the future.

A cold wind suddenly swept in across the cemetery grounds, coming from the direction of the farming complex, some six miles away toward the Great Rear Wall of the ship. Alcyone glanced in that direction. The

Great Rear Wall was faintly visible as a smoky grey, circular disc that towered thirty four degrees in angular elevation, going just over a third of the way up into the sky. That was not a true 'sky' of course...merely the opposite landscape of the cylindrical interior.

As the winds gathered pace, she noticed the tall pine trees nearby swaying from side to side, making their shadows dance eerily across the graveyard's surreal looking, dimly lit landscape. Overhead, thunder clouds rolled across the dark middle ground of the sky, looking up toward the opposite side of the ship. The dim lighting all around her created an impression of lower temperatures, which added to the chill in the air.

Alcyone suddenly felt quite uneasy about her present location...the thought of being surrounded by only the dead in this huge graveyard - and miles away from any civilisation - brought on a hint of fear to her heart. She recalled reading an article that said somewhere between seventy to a hundred consecutive generations laid buried in this place, having lived out their entire lives from cradle to grave on this great voyage to New Earth. Overgrowth of lichen on many of the more dated headstones and the mossy borders between graves, certainly echoed back the age of the place. As if to add to the morbid air, she now had a vivid recollection of the evil creatures that tormented her during sleep over the past couple of nights. These thoughts made her shudder, as she hurried on toward the graveyard's exit.

Occasional flashes of silent lightning lit up the dim landscape in a silvery glow. Granite headstones with glossy textures were intermittently set ablaze. There was no thunder to accompany the overhead lightning, only silence that was punctuated by sounds from the chilling breeze.

Alcyone remembered her wristcom, and frantically flicked through its channel selections.

'Joey! Do you read me?' She cried out across the airwaves.

A rather long, ten seconds of unsettling silence elapsed.

'Hey I read you. You sound distressed though, is everything okay?'

Alcyone felt hugely relieved, seeing his cute face appear on the tiny screen at last. She felt as if he were speaking from a million miles away.

'I'm at the cemetery and I just feel a little uneasy. Can you keep on talking please, I could do with a little company.' She was desperate for some human touch.

'Sure. Why the cemetery, thought you'd be at Caroline's?'

'I took a detour. Where are you right now?'

'I'm visiting an old friend of mine across the opposite side from you. I'll speak to you in a bit.'

Joey broke off his consultation with the mystic.

'Sorry to sound rude, Mr. Yurchenko, but I need to go outside for a couple of secs.'

He stood on the stretch of clear ground in front of Yurchenko's house, and lifted his head to peer up into the sky. Looking six miles directly overhead, he saw an aerial view of the cemetery across to the starship's opposite side, with its dimly lit graveyard appearing scattered across a rectangular patch.

The cemetery grounds from this distance appeared as a greyish clearance, surrounded by pine forests. Nearby, was the ever meandering Eridanus river, whose waters looked decidedly greenish from here, reflecting the midday simulated sunshine.

Joey looked at his wristcom. The 'laser' function was an additional piece of electronic gadgetry built into every wristcom as a standard feature. It could generate a variable beam of laser light, with a wide range of uses. On one extreme end of the scale, it could converge the beam to a piercingly sharp focus that could burn things or even serve as a short range weapon. On the opposite end of its range, it was used for pointing to objects as well as signalling to people over large distances across the curving landscape of the interior.

Joey switched the function of his wristcom to laser mode and adjusted its beam width and intensity. He angled the beam upwards toward the overhead graveyard, its rays scattering over a wide area which just about covered the width of the half a mile-wide by one mile-long, cemetery grounds.

'Look directly above you. Do you see where I'm at?'

Alcyone looked up into the sky as told, and saw the brilliant silver glow of Joey's flashing laser beam. Its luminous sparkle stood out like a beacon against the aerial view of the surrounding pine forest, which looked a vaguely bluish colour, past the dark sky in the foreground.

'You're inside the deep, dark, foreboding territory of the Black Forest? Careful you don't get eaten by an anaconda!' Alcyone said, humorously.

She adjusted her own wristcom to laser mode, and levelled it up into the sky.

'Here's me.'

'Your beam looks weak, think the batteries are on their way out. By the way, anacondas don't 'eat' people. They kill their victims by constriction,' Joey corrected her.

'So don't get 'constricted' then, mister.'

5. Chaos in the chain of command

Comet C-336

Credit: www.headstartproject.org

Joey was at work in the starship's main control room inside the Navigation and Control Complex, located east of Utopia. Having finished his scheduled tasks for the day, he was playing a game of virtual tennis with CPC.

Due to the constantly changing gravity vectors in the rotating ship, games such as tennis, baseball, football, along with anything else that involved propelling objects upwards or across the air, were made rather difficult. An object thrown upwards would hardly ever land at the intended spot back on the ground, since there was very little natural gravity to pull it down, and it was impossible to judge which part of the biosphere floor would 'catch up' to it in the ship's artificial gravity spin. Such games could therefore be only adequately played in virtual reality, i.e. on the computer.

On the control room's main screen, a forward view of the *Centauri Princess* was depicted in real time, showing a bright yellowish star at its centre, shining brilliantly against the black sky. That of course was Alpha Centauri, the ultimate destination goal of the mission. As the ship rotated in its artificial gravity spin, the stars surrounding Alpha Centauri appeared to describe circular paths around it, taking nearly two and a half minutes to complete one full revolution on the screen.

Not far from Joey, sat Zayna, the ship's in-flight mining coordinator. She was of Arabic descent by Earth origins, in her late twenties with midnight black hair and sharply defined, attractive features. She was browsing *Centauri Life* - a popular women's magazine that was the *Centauri Princess'* equivalent of the *Cosmopolitan*; her being highly looks conscious and vanity oriented. She wore strong perfume, that lingered in the control room's still air.

'We could do with adding an extra kiloton of H2O to reserves, seeing that Beta's descent module has been ready for despatch onto the surface of Comet C dash 336 for some time,' she said to Sharuk Rashid, looking up the info on CPC's console screen in front of her.

The starship was due to fly past a small comet, seen coming up ahead. The frozen water that covered its outer surface was a priceless commodity for topping up the starship's life support resources along the voyage.

A few feet away, Sharuk sat back in his chair and sipped decaffeinated coffee. He was looking over the ship's current resource status and pondering over needs for mining the comet.

'Scheduled rendezvous with C dash 336 in twenty five days and four point six hours. I say we skip this one; Gamma, further up ahead, has a higher payload and you know how filled to capacity we were the last time we refuelled prior to a level one alert,' he muttered to Zayna.

Zakarov entered the silent control room and glanced briefly at Sharuk with glaring eyes, on account of the manner in which he had broken up with Caroline, although he kept his smart, professional composure. He went to Joey's work station.

'Winning or losing?' He asked over Joey's shoulders, who was absorbed in stiff concentration with the computer game.

'Winning. By far,' he casually muttered, not looking away from the screen.

'When you have a moment, I'd like an update on the Eridanus banks in the Lower Province, please,' Zakarov said, and took the seat next to Joey.

There had been reports of rising water levels of Eridanus in the swampy region close to the Hardware Storage complex in the Lower Province, such that the banks could become flooded. Zakarov was concerned that any such overflow would cause damage to the newly cultivated pineapple plantations nearby. The fertile soils in that region offered the right blend of nutrients for successful pineapple cultivation, which had proved to be a difficult fruit to grow inside the main farming complex. This was in part to do with the species having been highly hybridised and not adequately adapted for the complex growing conditions onboard the ship.

Joey put the game on the console to pause and turned his swivel chair to face Zakarov.

'Everything looked fine on Saturday's cruise that Als and I went on. There was plenty of dry ground between

Eridanus and the lake opposite Hardware Storage,' he reported with certainty.

'Thanks Joey. Keep up the good work,' Zakarov praised, winking his left eye with hint of a smile.

'Did you manage to sort the weatherbot over the farming complex?' Joey asked.

'All fixed.'

Zakarov marched out of the control room just as swiftly as he had arrived.

'Thinks he's in charge of every god damn thing on this ship nowadays. A'int that the job of the Environmental office?' Sharuk said bitterly.

'He's looking for a promotion,' Zayna said humorously, making her and Joey chuckle.

'Technically, monitoring levels of rainfall and flood control via correct balance of thermals and electrostatics, does fall into Zakarov's remit,' Joey acknowledged. 'I'm off to the canteen, grab a bite to eat. I'll see you guys in there,' he said and rushed off.

'Wait. I'll join you.' Zayna followed him out, leaving Sharuk all to himself.

Sharuk was very much in line for promotion, having served well - or at least he thought that way about his own work - over the past five years as the chief navigation officer. But now there were rumours that could endanger all that. Zakarov had been spending more and more time in control room affairs lately, and his face showed up far too often for Sharuk's liking. Rumours had it that Zakarov would be transferred across to take command, threatening Sharuk's promotion prospects in a very big way.

Multi-tasking and job rotations were common themes

operated on the *Centauri Princess* going all the way back to her launch days from Earth. With a total crew and passenger make-up varying anywhere between eight hundred and three thousand people on the ship, having a highly flexible and multi-skilled workforce through an active program of job rotations was a core policy of the HR department. Amongst many other benefits, job rotation kept motivation levels up and made the day to day roles that much more interesting in this enclosed small world, where boredom would have been otherwise a major shortcoming. With such a small population, people were encouraged to learn more than one skill, and they often felt inclined to do so.

The fact that Sharuk had now found a better lover in someone other than Caroline was hardly his fault. But having said that, he did have a long history of short term relationships, and now Zakarov's niece was widely viewed as having been overtly and unscrupulously dumped by him. This made his working relationship with Zakarov all the more strained and bitter. And how long could he keep this new relationship a secret? Strict rules of conduct did forbid the pairing-off of people working closely within the same function, especially one as critical as starship navigation. If he had found out about such a liaison, it would be a virtual certainty that Zakarov would push hard for displacing Sharuk from the promotions list. Especially given his having the upper hand with superior technical experience as well.

Unless…Sharuk thought long and hard and remembered that he and Zakarov had both worked on a project that involved re-programming the resource scheduling module of CPC about five years back.

Zakarov was in charge then and had led that software upgrade with his superior technical acumen. Now...if Sharuk could somehow show that Zakarov had made a major screw up on that assignment, then this might help to taint his credentials a bit. But just *how* could one go about doing something like that?

He pondered that question for a while, and at last had an idea.

Speaking into the computer's voice input port, he said, 'CPC, I'd like access to the programming files on the resource scheduling module, please.'

'Sharuk, those are in the restricted archives and access can only be granted through the menus in front of you. Please follow the authentication instructions on the screen,' CPC replied in a half natural, monotone voice.

Sharuk looked through the menus in CPC's restricted archives area, and skimmed through various options until he reached the 'resource requirements planning module'. He began studying the manual that accompanied the module very long and hard.

Suddenly he heard footsteps in the corridor outside, coming towards the control room. They grew louder and heavier, coming from someone of a plump build, he thought. He hurried through the menus and resumed viewing pages with which he had routinely worked as Lucy, the telecoms officer, walked in.

'Hi Sharuk. How's it going? You look pretty engrossed in whatever you're doing there.'

'Hey Lucy. I'm just running a few manual checks on the resource status reported by CPC, make sure everything's ticking away nicely,' he said, briefly glancing up at her.

'Well that don't sound too taxing. Where are the others?'

'Over in the canteen, I believe.'

'Right. I think I'll go join them,' she said, and left.

Lucy was a key member of the control room. She was in her mid thirties, had short blonde hair and a plump build. As with most of her other colleagues, her role was highly varied with main emphasis being on keeping all aspects of electronic communications smoothly flowing around the ship.

As she left the control room, Sharuk resumed his quest for refamiliarisation with the resource scheduling module's intricate access paths. As with every other part of CPC's critical functions, the module had complex authentication verification requirements. This was as part of its security enforcement, making it next to impossible for anyone without the proper authorisation to gain access.

Late in the day, just after five thirty, the control room was gradually deserted, as one by one, the small crew making up the navigation team, started to go home.

'See you in the morning,' said Zayna.

'And tonight?' Sharuk asked, in a dry voice.

'I'll have to see.' Zayna was the last to go, leaving Sharuk all to himself once more.

In the course of that afternoon, he had managed to educate himself about the procedures both he and Zakarov had used all those years back to gain administrative access to the resource scheduling module's programming area. At last he felt he was ready, having adequately deciphered all the necessary steps. He only had one chance to get this right. For if CPC suspected anything was even remotely adrift from the norm, alarm bells could ring and he would be in big trouble.

'Please enter authentication sequence in its entirety:' Prompted CPC on the screen, the script appearing as an animated ticker. Sharuk typed in Zakarov's unique identifier, whose identity he assumed for this task: 'Code 034T' then 'Authentication ID := REPROG 4X7TP.' There then followed a complex series of entry requirements, that Sharuk keyed in meticulously. He felt relieved to see the 'Access granted' prompt from CPC at last.

One by one, he skilfully altered the variables that triggered different levels of alerts, such that there would be a delayed response when the ship's resource reserves would run low - particularly for water. Finally, to thoroughly cover his tracks and make the changes look as if they were done five years earlier when the project had been 'live', Sharuk altered the document change dates to match those of other files active at that time.

He knew that only Zakarov could ever suspect something was wrong, but he would never be able to provide sufficient proof to point the finger in Sharuk's direction. When they got to find out, the Mission Management Committee would thus have a *prima facie* case against Zakarov, for his technical incompetency in programming the module. With all the intricate tinkerings successfully completed, Sharuk exited the module and quietly left the control room for the day.

Two weeks later

Zakarov was at home, resting flat on his back on the sofa, both hands clasped behind his head. He stared up at the lounge's blank ceiling, and generally pondered about the state of affairs as of late. His suburban town house, nestled away in the pine forests a couple of miles to the west of Utopia, was silent, apart from the twittering of a few birds in the trees outside. Bright sunshine flooded in through the half open window, nearby. The room was partially shaded by long, burgundy coloured curtains that gently fluttered in the late afternoon breeze. He sensed a hint of sweet fragrance in the room, coming from the lilac flowers of a syringa plant that bloomed outside.

Quite a few thoughts floated around in his mind, although most of them were pleasant. He was satisfied with the job that he had done on the farming complex's weatherbot, restoring rainfall to normality over the past couple of weeks. And he was quite relieved since hearing Joey's favourable report on the status of river banks in the Lower Province. Pineapples were a sought after fruit across the communities, and their yields would be secure for next year's harvests. Meanwhile, Caroline had found a new direction at last, knowing more or less what she wanted out of life. Everything seemed to be going rather smoothly. Too smoothly, he thought.

With the sereneness that surrounded him, and the soothing late afternoon breeze flowing in from the woods outside, he felt himself gradually drifting off towards an afternoon kip…

Moments later, Zakarov tossed and turned in his sleep. Suddenly, he had found himself *there*. Where so many others had described themselves as having been before. On one of the phantom observation decks. Now it was his turn. It was dark, and he sensed it must have been in the depths of night inside the ship, as his surroundings were minutely illuminated by the feeble light from stars shining through the deck's glazed window. He wasn't sure for what purpose he'd been summoned to the Upper Province's observation deck in this dream state that he presently found himself in. The Milky Way's core gently glided across the glazed portal, as he looked out. The diffused light from a few hundred billion suns shone simultaneously onto his retina. Though, by virtue of great distance and the surrounding vacuum, that star-filled glow never cast more illumination than could be experienced on the darkest, moonless nights anywhere back here on Earth.

And then he began to see the phantom creatures arriving from the dark that shrouded the lonely ark ship all around. At first, he was trying to figure out exactly what they were. *What were they made up of? Material or energy or both? Where did they come from? Was there a reason for their attack? Was there a message?* Zakarov had asked himself those questions in his awake state so many times before having heard eye witness accounts from others, but he had never envisaged that he would be having to ask them in his dream state too.

Following what must have been several minutes of the cloud of darkness gradually taking on the shape of the five menacing beasts, a horrifying chase began in his nightmare. Zakarov found himself running for his life toward the elevator, along the dimly lit corridor. As he ran, he occasionally turned back and tried firing the laser beam from his wristcom, having adjusted it to lethal levels of intensity. But as he fully expected, that was to very little avail. The beam seemed to go right through the bodies and wings of the phantom creatures; they were, after all, merely dream images within the dream itself, devoid of any substance. But somehow, they were more than that. What was so astonishingly perplexing…was that the merciless beasts appeared to be *physical* at the same time…

By the time he had reached the elevator, Zakarov was forced into a brawl with the leader, the archangel in the pack of five, which had caught up with him. Although the four trailing beasts were much less vigorous in their attack, one of them managed to deliver a vicious blow, digging its razor-sharp nails into Zakarov's right shoulder through the tough fabric of the commander's uniform which he wore. This left a series of open wounded scars, pouring out blood.

With a knife stabbing pain emanating from the wounds, the battle scene suddenly faded from Zakarov's mind, after which he found himself fully awake once again, panting audibly on the sofa where he lay in the dark room. The automated lighting system around the house had the hall way lamp outside, fully turned on. Its rays flooded into the lounge where Zakarov had slept. He realised at once that he must have been either hallucinating or perhaps he had only momentarily crossed that uncertain dividing line between awake and sleep? No, he must have been fully asleep, he figured. And for much longer than that. For he could see it was dark outside, through the lounge's window, whose curtains were only partially drawn.

He glanced up at the clock on the far wall, and was surprised when it dawned on him that he had been gone for at least *four hours*. He had a vivid recollection of the nightmare and felt relieved that it was only that - a nightmare. Except, that is, when he looked at his right shoulder...there was blood oozing from a series of scars, where he remembered one of the nightmare's wolf angels had managed to deliver a scratching blow during the scuffle - in his dream.

'What the heck!' He exclaimed and made a dash for the first aid box in the kitchen, toward the back of the house.

On a four wheel drive, open top rover, a park ranger was going about his day to day patrols in a pine forest, several miles away from Utopia. He had an ancestry that linked him back to Central Africa by Earth origins. Given the vast expanse of rain forests and open savannahs that prevailed in that region of our planet, he was naturally from a background well suited to the present role of park ranger within the miniature world. As a matter of fact, park rangering was in his blood; his father had been a park ranger, who happened to have superseded his grandfather in that same line of work, a few generations earlier.

On this beautiful morning, as he briskly steered his vehicle through the dense forest, he was humming and whistling to a series of hymns playing on his rover stereo. He frequently listened to hymn tracks on his patrols. Not that he was a particularly religious man or anything, he just liked the melodic way the vocals and tunes were performed. 'Morning has broken' poured out of the speakers, which was sung by a female soloist from a choir in his local church, in the lower eastern suburbs of Utopia. Beams of early morning sunshine filtered down through the thick overhead foliage, and the mood of the song nicely suited the surroundings. Unlike the lyrics in the hymn, however, there were no 'black birds speaking', although there were other song birds thriving here that did speak out at this hour of the day.

As he drove on, he noticed this part of the forest floor was carpeted with a fine display of late flowering bluebells. They were still covered in early morning dew, and stretched out as a thin layer of blue mist in all directions. The evergreen conifers that towered above had dark brown bark shrouding their enormous trunks. They were grooved-in by strangling strands of thick ivy, that hinted at great age. Many of these trees were truly ancient; as old as the voyage itself in fact, having been planted by the first generation whilst the starship was still docked into orbit around planet Earth. The larger varieties were a special adaptation of their giant Earthly cousins, like the *Sequoiadendron Giganteum*s of the mighty Californian redwoods, growing along the western slopes of the Sierra Nevada.

Eventually, the forest thinned out and the ranger reached a gladed opening. He brought the rover to a juddering halt, and scanned the landscape over to his right.

Something was wrong.

Some of the trees were looking decidedly parched and

unhealthy. Fallen pine needles had settled into a carpet of brown mulch, which covered the forest floor. He was slightly alarmed, and pondered about the cause. Experience told him that it was most likely down to lack of water in the underground reservoirs, which fed the tree roots when they needed to quench their thirst. He grabbed a clipboard from the glove compartment of his vehicle and scribbled down some notes onto a reporting sheet.

Driving up the road, the ranger filed his findings at the Environmental office, where Alcyone and a small group of co-ecosystems researchers were working.

'Don't look too good at all. You may want to alert Zakarov and the MMC,' he said, and left the office to carry on with the rest of his patrols that day.

Continuing on his travels, he noticed a large chunk of the forests west of Utopia showed signs of an impending drought. He recalled the last time when anything on this scale had affected the scenic beauty of his patrols, was a long time ago. More than a decade earlier, in fact. That was when a forest fire, started inadvertently by a group of teenagers camping out in the woods, had gone wildly out of control. That incident had devastated as much as five per cent of the miniature world's woodlands, momentarily upsetting the delicate ecosystem balance. The destroyed trees then had to be gradually regrown, and they still had a long way to go before completely restoring the balance.

Zakarov drove into the parking lot at the back of the Medical Facility building in central Utopia, and parked

Betty as soon as he had found a vacant space in the congested lot. He entered the building through sliding doors at its rear, and continued along the long, tunnel-like corridor.

Eventually he reached the large open foyer, where the reception area was sited. Caroline worked as a senior nurse in this section, and she was showing a new graduate trainee the basics of Med admin procedures. Just then, out of the corner of her eye, she was surprised to see Zakarov coming over. It was rare for him to visit the Med. Something was wrong.

'Continue as you are, I'll only be a moment,' Caroline said to the trainee.

She left him on his own and rushed over.

'Unc. Good to see you, is everything okay?' She asked, with a slightly concerned look.

'Not quite. Is Gordon about?' Zakarov said, sounding urgent.

She noticed the bandage on his right shoulder, as he unbuttoned his shirt.

'My god. What happened?'

'Don't ask. Those darn nightmares are now starting to get *physical*,' he exclaimed, taking the nearest seat.

'These look like…claw marks. But how?' She said, utterly bewildered.

Just then, a rather smart looking character, wearing the Med's standard attire of a long, white jacket for male doctors, entered the foyer from across the other side. He took brisk steps to reach the area where Zakarov was seated.

'What on earth happened to you man?'

'We're not on earth Gordon, thought I told you to get the lingo straight,' Zakarov replied humorously.

'Nightmares,' Caroline said.

Gordon Crista was the *Centauri Princess'* chief medical officer. He was forty five, and had a slick, businesslike profile. With light brown hair and a narrow face, he was a gentle character, although his outward appearance implied a lot more seriousness.

Crista made a close examination of the wounds.

'We've got a worsening epidemic on our hands, but this is the first instance of anything physical,' he acknowledged.

'Thought you experts at the Med would be on top of a firm diagnosis by now. Damn it Gordon, what the hell is going on?' Zakarov said, sounding annoyed.

'We did send out statements over personal wristcoms and made TV announcements alerting folks to keep as many lights on around their homes as possible, throughout the hours of darkness.'

'Well that is hardly a diagnosis. As you know full well, we have to maintain a natural night cycle for the plants and vegetation growing across the biosphere; we cannot adopt a starship-wide 'lights on' policy at night,' Zakarov said. 'I want you people to get a fast handle on what these things are, where they come from, what the hell they want from us and what the heck we can do to scare them away!'

Crista came closer and lowered his voice, to try and dramatise his message.

'Look Zakarov, this is now very serious. I have a feeling that what we're dealing with here is a little outside the realm of our known medical science. How shall I explain this—' he said, pausing to gather his thoughts.

He continued, 'These creatures appear to be operating as beings of pure energy, possibly existing in some alternate dimension that is separate from our own, and it seems there is no way we can fight them on a material plane that is common to both our world and theirs.'

'Are you saying this is a *spiritual* phenomenon?' Zakarov couldn't take down what he was hearing.

'I am saying this is a complex phenomenon that needs an alternative angle of investigation.'

Zakarov gave him a look.

'Great. I've been scratched by the claws of one of these god damn beasts and they're not physical. So what do you suggest?'

Crista paused for a moment again, gathering his thoughts.

'Ever heard of a guy named Karim Yurchenko?'

'Nope.' Zakarov replied, bluntly.

'He calls himself a 'mystic', although he has a substantial background in psychology. From what Joey was telling me yesterday, Yurchenko could be our man for getting some intimate answers using an unconventional angle of inquiry. I would encourage you to pay him a visit.'

Caroline had replaced the bandage on Zakarov's right shoulder with a fresh one that was more adequate in fully covering the gruesome looking wounds. His wristcom bleeped faintly, as a message was registered. He stood up and buttoned the upper half of his shirt.

'I'm needed in the control room. I have got to dash,' he said, checking the message on his wristcom.

In the control room, Sharuk read the message from the Environmental office on the dire status of H_2O resources, but chose to ignore it for now. Let things get even worse, he thought. Instead of addressing the resource issues, he casually continued with his other duties of charting the forward path and getting a fix on the relative distances, light times and ship-relative velocities of comets and planetoids sensed in the hundred astronomical units radius sphere surrounding the *Centauri Princess*. To make this visual, CPC projected a scaled-down graphic of the vast 3D environment onto the main screen, that was universally viewable by everyone inside the control room.

Zayna was chewing gum and manicuring her nails, as she sat at her work station, clearly unaware of any immediate resource emergencies.

Sharuk's wristcom bleeped with a call from Zakarov.

'What's our present H_2O status, according to CPC?' He asked.

'I got a message from Alcyone at Environmental saying the trees are looking kinda sickly, but CPC is saying we're well within limits for even a level one alert to have been raised. It's kind of puzzling.'

'I'm on my way in. Something just doesn't sound right,' Zakarov closed the conversation.

Here on Earth, natural processes within our ecosystem ensure continuous recycling of water across the vast biosphere of our planet, with the whole system functioning as a self-contained unit to provide the necessary conditions for life to flourish. Additional input of water from external sources across the vast aeons of time that our world has been sustaining life was, quite possibly, never needed. I emphasize 'possibly', because some scientists have argued that the water levels in the biosphere of planet Earth could actually be continually being topped up by small comets entering the upper atmosphere and adding their water content, as our world encounters them on its travels through space.

Still others have argued that since we cannot physically detect these miniature comets colliding with our upper atmosphere, do they really exist? Instead, volcanoes throwing out vast quantities of water vapour up into the sky could account for replenishment of any such vapour possibly seeping away into space.

Water replenishment within the 'miniature Earth' environment inside the *Centauri Princess*, was deemed to be necessary right from the outset. The mission's design blueprint was structured accordingly, since, even under the most tightly managed experimental scenarios, the overall recycling efficiency of this crucial resource was found to be tangibly below one hundred per cent. This meant losses would need to be recovered by mining water-rich comets found en-route, along the voyage. Unlike the Earth, however, losses of water vapour in the context of the starship did not amount to physical seepage out into space, since the body of the ship was, quite literally, watertight. Rather, here the losses were due to transformation into non-water based compounds; for every one hundred molecules of water evaporating up into the sky from the river and lakes, perhaps only ninety nine of them would condense into water vapour to form clouds that eventually returned back to the ground as rainfall and other forms of precipitation. One molecule would occasionally be lost somewhere along the way. The likelihood was, over countless years of such accumulating losses, replenishment of water from external sources would become necessary.

Success of the mission thus heavily depended on maintaining a series of large navigation platforms (alpha, beta, gamma, etc.) operating at various distances ahead of the ship, that served as critical 'trailblazers'. They continually sensed the 3D space environment and sent back telemetry reports on upcoming cometary bodies. CPC received these reports and autonomously weighed up the forward resource availability against projected requirements, based on current usage. The navigation team oversaw that decision process, and determined if any minor course corrections would be needed for the starship to either dodge a particular resource island - if it posed a head-on collision hazard - or successfully mine it in advance or even rendezvous with it. To facilitate such tactics, the *Centauri Princess* was of course adequately equipped with a set of giant pitch/yaw, roll and retro thrusters that enabled full three-axis orientation and manoeuvrability control during each encounter phase. As replenishment of water became necessary, each of the giant navigation platforms operating ahead of the ship was equipped with its own descent module, which could be dispatched well in advance for in-situ mining operations on the surface of the comet. The mined resources would then be retrieved via a rendezvous with the descent module's upper stage that autonomously delivered the cargo into the shuttle EVA bay, as the ship flew past the comet.

Should there have been any failures with the navigation platforms or their descent modules, the mission design had a secondary, backup method for in-flight resource mining. This would involve launching a cluster of missiles from a bay at the front of the ship which would disintegrate the comet ahead, causing its material to become ionised. Then a magnetic funnel, erected around the body of the starship, would simply 'scoop up' the ionised material, as the ship flew through the debris cloud. However, this method of resourcing the starship's life support needs was expected to be comparatively less efficient, since the ionised plasma would need reconstituting into normal matter via in-house processes, with some losses inevitable along the way. For this reason, that was only a 'just in case', backup method, and it had never been used in practice - at least not so far into the voyage, anyway.

The navigation team, headed by Sharuk, oversaw all the calculations and monitored the results from all forward navigation instrument suites to ensure smooth mission progress. At this moment of course, things had been thrown a little adrift. Thanks to Sharuk's tinkering with the resource scheduling module, CPC did not issue an advance refuelling alert and the starship's biosphere reserves were running dangerously dry...

Zakarov knew that any failures in the planning module would likely be thoroughly investigated by the

MMC, and directly attributed to him. Since he was the one who had led the project to completely revamp the module and upgrade its software all those years back. He therefore needed to handle this pretty sensitively. *But just how could CPC's planning module have failed to issue a level one alert in time?*

Since the upgrade, the ship had performed one minor refuelling rendezvous with a comet some years earlier, although that was prior to any alerts being raised; merely on a 'let's grab some resource while we can, could be useful' kind of basis. Of course! It could only be Sharuk, Zakarov thought. He remembered how they had shared a common authentication ID on the project. *That son of a bitch is behind this, and I know it.* Zakarov also knew of course, he could prove nothing.

Continuing on his day to day patrols, the *Centauri Princess'* park ranger drove into the Wildlife Preserve in the Upper Province, where the vast majority of the miniature world's more exotic species of animals roamed in their natural habitats. The vegetation here was mixed; from isolated fir trees, similar to the ones commonly found in mid-northern latitudes here on Earth, to densely-packed bamboo forests that projected their tall spires way up into the sky. The Preserve was designed to encompass as much of the wide ranging vegetation and animal habitats, found across all the separate continents of Earth, as possible.

Just *how* you tightly package such wide ranging flora and fauna from the vast, subtropical regions from all the continents of planet Earth into a small area of no more than ten to fifteen square miles…and keep the whole thing naturally flourishing at the same time…was a major challenge for the starship's MMC in the early years of the voyage. As things started to naturally adapt over time, and the habitats developed more in harmony with the rest of the starship's ecosystem, upkeep of the wildlife sanctuary gradually became a lot more easier to manage.

The road that trailed across the centre of the Preserve was barely more than a dirt track in places, and as seen from the perspective of someone driving along it, it looked to be curving upwards toward the 'sky' as it ran laterally along the starship's curved interior.

As the park ranger made more progress on his travels, he looked across to the left hand side of the trail route. Over in the distance, he saw a small herd of spotted deer emerge into a narrow opening; they eyed him from the edge of their miniature rain forest habitat. This particular breed of deer had their origins in the subtropical *Sundarbans* region back on Earth, and had been specially bred and adapted on the ship mainly for gaming purposes. That became popular during the winter season.

A few hundred yards over to his right, he examined the state of the Preserve's main water feature. Ordinarily that would have been a large, shallow pool of muddy water that provided a natural habitat for the pink flamingo population. Its levels were maintained by underground pipelines that supplied water in balance with the rate at which the liquid evaporated up into the sky to form clouds and rainfall, mirroring the natural evaporation and condensation cycles we observe here on Earth.

Presently, due to the reserves drying out in the underground tanks, no water could be supplied and the ranger saw how bone dry the flamingo habitat looked. *Now, where had they all flocked to?* He wondered. Just then, there was a kind of faintly pulsating, hissing sound coming from the sky above, over to his left.

'Oh there you are, birds!' He said and beamed.

Peering up, he saw the vast expanse of pink scattered across the sky, as the flamingos flew overhead on their forced migratory path towards lakes and wider stretches of Eridanus river in the Lower Province.

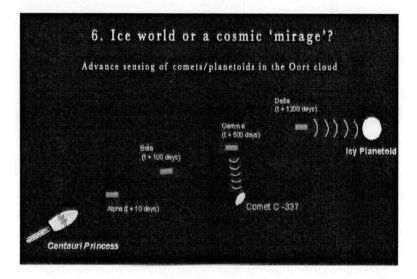

6. Ice world or a cosmic 'mirage'?

Advance sensing of comets/planetoids in the Oort cloud

Zakarov marched into the main control room, determined to put his full authoritative weight into resolving the resource issues. He was a natural born leader and always had an air of invincibility about him. It was at moments like this, that his leadership qualities shone through brightest.

'Right, first things first. What is the status of Beta's descent module?' He asked Zayna, completely ignoring Sharuk.

'Technically, we would be a little too late to retrieve Beta's upper stage with a full load, as the rendezvous window is gone,' she replied, chewing gum.

'What are our expediting options? We need those one point two kilotons of H2O, as emergency. Please issue the dispatch command *now*,' he said in a stern, no-nonsense voice, glancing toward Sharuk.

Sharuk just hated that superior commanding tone. Ordinarily, he would have made some kind of sarcastic gesture in response, but this time he did not want to kick up a fuss. He did not have to. If the resource scheduling module's failures were any signs to go by, then he had set into motion the right measures to keep Zakarov in his place. He quietly entered the command on the console, as instructed.

'Expediting costs fuel and we'll get far less now since the lead time is that much shorter. We might retrieve twenty five percent below optimum, if we're lucky,' Sharuk pointed out.

'Should be just about okay to take us to the next island. What is the latest schedule for that?' Zakarov asked.

'Comet C dash 337 was sensed by Gamma about a month ago. Although it will offer a higher payload potential, happens to be as much as two degrees off our present course line and CPC is not recommending that to be economical for mining. Further up ahead, the Delta nav platform has identified an icy planetoid, roughly the size of Earth's Moon in diameter. Our ETA with that island projected to be in just over three years - that's the earliest,' briefed Zayna.

'Well if we can recover a minimum of seven hundred tons from C dash 336, then we would be covered for at least five years, which would take us nicely past Delta's planetoid,' said Zakarov.

Joey struggled to keep any sort of confidence in Zayna's report, given the system issues as of late. He'd been following the conversations intently up till now, waiting for the right moment to have his say.

'With all the hiccups as of late, how do we know that CPC is not seeing a 'mirage' through its forward sensors on the Delta platform?' He remarked, rather abruptly.

Zayna looked at him and frowned.

'No, the planetoid is no mirage - as you put it Joey. It was initially sensed by the Epsilon platform over a year ago. A pretty *real* source of water-ice, and a big one at that I can assure you,' she said, giving him a look.

'Two platforms operating independently of each other can't both be wrong. Regardless of that though, from now on, please override the planning module's recommendations until further notice. We simply cannot afford any more let downs. I will be going over the software upgrade shortly,' Zakarov said. 'Delta's ice world will require us to make a full stopover, on an orbital rendezvous. Not necessarily a bad thing, we could pick up other vital resources there too.'

'We don't *have to* make a full stopover. Think of the zillions of tons of fuel losses to bring this giant tatonka to a complete stop. In case anyone's forgotten, there is also the small mining ship option, if only we weren't going to piss in our pants at the very thought of high speed EVA trips,' Sharuk snapped.

'Right. You're being nominated to present this to the MMC. But first, we need to nail the reasons why the planning module played up in the first place,' Zakarov said - very suggestively - and marched out of the control room to work from home.

'I saw them winged things again last night,' Irene said to her mum, as she chewed breakfast cereal sat in the large, wooden kitchen.

'Oh sweetie, how dreadful. Why didn't you wake me

up? I hope they weren't too mean to you,' Rujina said with feeling.

Irene shook her head.

'I guess it's loss of sleep that bugs me the most.'

'Tell you what. We'll go pay a visit to the Med today.'

'Think they'll cure it?'

'I don't know sweetie. We just need to be positive, okay?'

'Okay.'

'Hurry on up and finish your breakfast.'

Rujina was twenty eight and had loosely flowing, reddish brown hair and a slender complexion. Presently, she was using a miniature vacuum cleaner to rid the dust off of a few items of antiques, that lined the window sill toward the back of the kitchen. They were inherited from her father's distinguished antiques career. When the shuttle disaster killed both their parents over a decade earlier, Alcyone and Rujina had inherited their wealthy estate in a fifty-fifty split, as the only surviving offspring. This beautiful house in Midsummer Crescent was part of that inheritance, and Rujina felt even more grateful for it now, as a single parent, having to bring up her only child all by herself.

Having heard about Irene's latest nightmares, she had a worried look on her face. At first, literally sticking to 'what the doctor ordered' about keeping lights on around the house seemed to do the trick. Lately though, it seemed her daughter's nightmares were becoming more frequent and harrowing. Even Tommy and Razia, two of Irene's friends who lived on the same street, were seeing things in their dreams. The syndrome was somehow affecting the younger generation a lot more than the older folk across the ship.

'Mom, please can we get aunty to come along? I'm a bit scared of what the doctor might put me through,' Irene pleaded.

'You've said it. I'll go call her.'

Rujina hoped that her sister would be able to have the morning off work. Since Alcyone had also experienced similar nightmares, it was understandable that Irene would not feel isolated in her consultation at the Med. Rujina went into the garden at the back of their house via the conservatory. Standing in the pristine, early morning sunshine, she called out on her wristcom.

'Hey Als, it's only me. Listen, I need to ask you a favour. Are you able to take the morning off work?'

'I think so. Why, what's up?'

'I am getting generally a bit concerned about Irene. Even keeping the house brightly lit all night, simply won't do it for us anymore and many of her friends in Midsummer Crescent are seeing the same things,' Rujina explained.

'We could take her to see a specialist at the Med.'

'Exactly my own thoughts, only she says she would feel more comfortable if you were around. She doesn't want to relive the bad experience in front of the doctors all by herself.'

'I can meet you both there at ten thirty,' Alcyone offered.

'Thanks, we'll see you there,' Rujina said, as her sister's video image faded from the wristcom.

Zakarov sat in the office room on the first floor of his town house, remotely logging into CPC's resource scheduling module. Virtually all of CPC's processing hardware was of course physically located inside the Navigation and Control Complex, over on the other side of Utopia. He grabbed a memory unit from a nearby cupboard that was headed 'RSP Programming' and slotted it into a port below the interactive screen. He went through the authentication procedures manually to reach the programming environment.

Looking through the variables list, he compared their base values against those recorded in the memory unit, and instantly spotted the differences. There was the answer to all the mishaps of late with failed alerts and so forth, he thought. He then observed that that was not all of the problems. When the base variables had been tampered with, the delicate balance of the whole system had been thrown into complete disarray, with CPC making erroneous compensations in some places that diverted water channelling away from other areas of the ship on a false premise. This must explain the sudden dry out of the flamingo habitat within the Wildlife Preserve, he thought.

Gritting his teeth with anger, Zakarov began on the long road to resetting the variables to what they ought to have been. He envisaged this to be a laborious process that could take several hours, at the very least. Once the base variables were restored and realigned, they would once again be perfectly calibrated to the real world model that took full account of the starship's wider ecosystem harmony, balancing usage rates against reserve levels and working on a feedback loop based on projected availability in the forward path of the ship.

Alcyone had been walking for about five minutes since getting off at Utopia Central, along a quiet back street on her way to the Med. That was when she spotted Sharuk's open top Corvette parked across on the other side of the street. Approaching from the back, she could see he was with someone and they were exchanging kisses inside the sportish looking rover. It was Zayna, she identified walking closer toward the vehicle. So that's the girl of his present, fleeting passions having dumped Caroline, she thought. Still it was none of her business, so she continued on the opposite sidewalk past the blue rover, pretending not to have noticed anything.

She wondered about the future her and Joey would have together, once they got married. The present state of her world, with relationships falling apart all around, did not inspire a great deal of confidence in Alcyone, even though he was sweet and they were in the depths of love. Okay, marriage was still working for most folks across Utopia, she acknowledged.

And what of Rujina's husband? Alcyone thought about her elder sister's marriage that fell into shambles two years earlier. That was another story altogether, she knew. He was a gambling addict with a drink problem, way outside permissible conduct and moral behaviour for a Muslim husband and a father to his only child, Irene. Rujina was now a single parent, but at least she had a more dignified life after breaking up with the guy. And Caroline's relationship with Sharuk? That was earmarked for failure right from the word go, but then no one could have guessed he was such a big womaniser in his secret life.

Once her thoughts wandered back to Joey though, Alcyone did not want to ponder the question any further. He was the one. Her knight in shining armour, and she felt very sure about that. She could say without reservation that being with him made her feel as elated with a complete sense of happiness and tranquility as anything she'd ever encountered in her most sweetest of dreams.

In the first two millennia of this great voyage, the *Centuari Princess'* closed-knit communities had gone through all extremes of social and moral behaviour. Initially, the individual communities were pretty orderly and well set in their structures, having had the highest regard for family values, stable marriages, and moderate religious doctrines that all worked in harmony with each other and with the broader goals of the one-way, multi-generational mission. However, further into the voyage, marriage had gradually began to lose its shine, with many sections of the ship moving towards cohabiting, open relationships, single parenting and the like. Equally, gays and lesbians had the freedom to do as they pleased and generally, society had moved into godlessness and lost most of its sound, moral footing.

That disorderly system could not go on forever though, and eventually began to wake people up to its fundamental flaws, with small pressure groups emerging, who had done 'before versus after' studies to show how things were a lot better in the good old days. Gradually, the various communities realised that having good moral standards, stable marriage and family structures were in the best interests of the mission as a whole, especially given the limited size of the overall population and the amount of space available across the interior.

Towards the middle of the second millennium, the MMC had began to implement a series of 'back to basics' campaigns that helped the various communities to work their way back toward the model with which the ship had departed from Earth. So much so that now, if a person was found sleeping around having passed the age of thirty, eyebrows would be raised and some gossip would be certain to be heard in at least one corner of Utopia. Sharuk and Caroline's present relationship failure was a prime example of that, even though she was only twenty four and he had barely turned thirty.

Rujina and Irene met up with Alcyone in the Med's foyer area as arranged. Caroline was there to greet them and they were then shown into the psychoanalysis and sleep therapy lab, going further into the building. Irene was asked to remove her existing clothes and change into a medical gown for the therapy session. Alcyone accompanied her into the changing room and helped her through that process. There was some uncertainty about jewellery and ornaments though, the instructions weren't too clear on whether the silver chain and sapphire-embedded pendant that Irene wore as a necklace, ought to be removed.

'That needs to come off too, I'm afraid,' Caroline said, looking in from around the other side of the partition.

Irene took off the necklace and handed it to Alcyone for safe keeping.

'When did you get this? I haven't seen you wearing it before,' she enquired.

'Daddy gave it to me. For my birthday when I was seven.'

'It's real pretty, and charming. I bet you're missing him a lot?'

Irene nodded. 'Hasn't visited mommy and me for about six months now.'

She put on the medical gown and they moved into the therapy lab.

Irene was told to lie down on the specialized, sleep monitoring bed. Tiny electrodes were then lightly attached, first onto her forehead, and then running across to either side of her skull. Each of these miniature wireless devices had sophisticated electronics that could scan her mind's 'eye' and sense a myriad of vital information, which included brain wave characteristics and dream images. They would then transmit the data across the room to a set of plasma screen monitors.

'There seems to be no obvious pattern or distinction in the brain waves which triggers the dark-induced nightmares from that of ordinary dreams,' Caroline said.

One of the section's senior professionals entered the sleep therapy lab. He introduced himself to the newcomers.

'Dr. Chang, can we actually get an image of the creatures that my daughter reports seeing in her nightmares?' Asked Rujina.

'Yes, theory says once intensity reaches a certain strength, we should pick up a image on the screens, here.' Chang said in his own style of talking, referring to the row of hi-tec monitor screens.

Frederick Chang was a stocky looking character, with a wide face and narrow eyes. He had an ancestry that linked him back to China, by Earth origins. In common with the Med's uniform policy for all male doctors, he wore a long, white coat that made him stand out in the small crowd.

As Irene's nightmare intensified, surely enough to everyone's utter amazement, a faint image of the creatures began to materialise on the monitor screens. The nightmare was allowed to continue for ten long minutes, as a vague outline of each entity, with its distinctive wings and head, became more easily discernible. Not surprisingly, the session was particularly painful for Rujina, who felt helpless as she watched her little girl go through the traumatic experience.

Meanwhile, Alcyone was astonished by what she saw.

'That's just too much of a coincidence. These bastards are kind of similar to what I've been seeing in my own nightmares for these past few weeks!' she exclaimed.

Caroline nodded with a sigh, 'It seems like a common theme right across the ship.'

Gordon Crista entered the room, carrying a large file of papers. He smiled as a greeting to the crowd and made a beckoning gesture to Chang, as he wandered across to the other side of the room. He opened the file and pulled out a colourful chart.

'Result from study you talk about?' Chang asked.

'I've examined the ship's historic records going back

over the past several hundred years, and we may be close to a firm diagnosis. There seems to be a strong correlation between the number of patients reporting bad dreams and how far we venture away from the Sun. As if the great enveloping cosmic dark around the ship is somehow interacting with our brain waves,' he explained, handing the chart to his most senior doctor.

The high levels of mysticism once a major part of human society not so long ago: spirits, ghosts, poltergeists, recurring nightmares,...all appear to have receded since invention of the electric light bulb and the higher levels of illumination that we now enjoy in modern times here on Earth. In this voyage, as the *Centauri Princess* headed deeper into dark space, the old mystical phenomena appeared to have naturally resurfaced. Or at least that is how the earlier generations up to this point in the voyage had interpreted milder versions of the so-called 'wolf angels syndrome' and lived with it.

'There seems to be an oscillation period of roughly eighty years within the nightmare trend though, which is both interesting and puzzling at the same time -' Crista muttered to himself, in a quieter tone, 'and we are now heading toward that eighty year peak again.'

Chang studied the chart and sighed. It resembled the price track of a bluechip stock; generally trending upwards, with sharper peaks and gentler troughs in the underlying oscillations.

'Interesting, that. I wonder if this have something with Alpha Centauri's binary set up? I think they orbit each other every eighty years too,' he said quietly, as the two men kept their distance from the rest of the group gathered around Irene's bedside.

They exchanged views and speculated on whether the two observations could be more than a simple coincidence. The two primary suns of the Alpha Centauri system do indeed take roughly eighty years to complete one circuit about their common centre of gravity. Chang was ready to put two and two together. Such risk-taking and bold deductions were perfectly normal and within his unique character.

'This theory rook really absurd and far-fetch...suppose that in some far advanced evolution, too much outside comprehension, alien race on planet of Alpha Centauri system have evolved capacity to project their images into space...No. Forget I said that...It's sounding like too absurd!'

Chang stopped himself and chuckled, fearing ridicule from his superior if he continued such a wild speculation.

Crista thought for a moment, looking directly at Chang. *Wait a minute. This guy might have problems with his English and the way he expresses himself in his profession, but boy...he sure does have some intuitive deduction capabilities.*

'It may be absurd and just a fanciful speculation, but that's how a lot of scientific theories are, when someone first thinks of them,' Crista reassured. 'We'll wait to hear what Zakarov finds out from our mystical man, Yurchenko, because he's been blabbing on about these so-called 'visions' that he's been getting along these lines for quite some time.'

By now, Caroline had fully awakened Irene from her short, medically induced sleep; the little girl sat up on the bed and yawned. Alcyone sat right next to her, just as she had done before Irene had fallen asleep.

As the consultation was coming to an end, Alcyone felt quite bitter about the lack of a real solution, and she knew that she had fared particularly badly as of late in her own nightmares. A very key question had been burning away deep down inside and was on the tip of her tongue for a while now. *To hell with what anybody thinks, I'm gonna ask it*, she thought.

'Dr. Chang, do you have any idea as to the *very worst* that these nightmare creatures can do to us? I mean, can they for example, kill or maim someone in their nightmare?

Crista cleared his throat and edged forward to intervene, as he felt this to be quite a sensitive and high profile topic that deserved a carefully balanced response. As a senior person on the MMC, he wanted to maintain an atmosphere of as much equanimity in the crisis, as possible.

'Young lady, in theory that can never happen, but let me explain how. You see the way it works is this. The creatures can interfere with a person's brain waves during sleep, and cause them to confront them in that state, inducing as much fear as possible in the nightmare. But the moment when the confrontation becomes physical and some pain is directly inflicted on the sleeping person, the body's natural reaction is to wake them up. This marks the limit of any physical harm.'

Alcyone thought for a moment. She could sort of agree with the logic of what he was saying.

'Okay, that's clearer now.'

She felt somewhat relieved and glad to have asked.

Although she caught onto the political sensitivity behind the subject by the tone of Crista's voice, and part of her still felt they didn't really know the full truth behind the syndrome's worst possibilities.

Rujina thanked Chang for giving them an insight into Irene's dreams, as they left the Med's foyer, although she too was left feeling dissatisfied with the service overall.

'Sorry we could not help more, but rest assured we are going to find a good fix on these symptom soon.' Chang said, sounding confident.

It's amazing how much confidence you can inspire in people with just your words, even though you actually deliver very little, Rujina thought.

A magnified image of Comet C dash 336 loomed large on the main viewing screen of the control room, as Sharuk and the rest of the navigation team watched.

At an eye watering distance of over a trillion miles from the Sun, the billion-tonne ball of rock and ice could not exhibit a dust or ionisation tail, which of course is a familiar feature with the comets we see in the night skies here on Earth. As such a space rock drifted in the cold, inky blackness of interstellar space, the only way it could be characterised as a 'comet' as opposed to an 'asteroid', would be based upon its surface composition; comets are 'dirty snowballs', made up of a loose mixture of frozen chemicals, rock and ice, as originally noted by Dr. Fred Whipple back in the 1950s. Asteroids, by comparison, are normally composed of hard rock or metal or a combination of the two.

Comet C dash 336 appeared to be shaped rather like a

potato and of very low surface brightness, as it slowly rotated in space. The dim surface brightness was to be expected of course; the total amount of starlight illuminating an object in local interstellar space, never amounted to more than a microscopic flux of one three hundredth of a full moon equivalent - *'Ahad's constant'*.

'The upper stage of the descent module should now be ready to lift-off for rendezvous with us, delivering its cargo of H_2O,' Zayna said.

'Telemetry reports show status is good, but the yield is disappointing.' Sharuk sounded pessimistic.

On the dark surface of Comet C dash 336, the upper stage of the surface mining pod ignited its main engines as its onboard computer executed a pre-programmed sequence. The frozen water-ice laden upper stage required very minimal amounts of thrust to escape the weak gravity of the comet. It adjusted its course as it rose higher up into sky to ensure it remained on track for a successful meet up with the *Centauri Princess*, during her close fly by of the comet. As reported by Beta's navigation sensors several weeks earlier, Comet C dash 336 measured three miles long by one and a half miles wide; potentially offering as much as twelve hundred tons of water-ice for adding to starship reserves. This limit was of course imposed by the limited payload capacity of Beta's descent module and its upper stage; in theory, one could mine countless times that quantity, given the substantial total mass of the comet.

A few hours later, the broadly rectangular shaped upper stage delivered its cryogenically frozen water content into the shuttle EVA bay in the Lower Province. From there, industrial robots autonomously liquefied and processed the resource, channelling it via pipe lines into the vast underground reserve tanks.

Late in the afternoon, Alcyone and her colleagues were watching TV in the lounge of the Environmental office, having completed most of their work for the day. Starship president Zed Lincoln appeared on the screen wearing a formal suit that bore the MMC logo. He issued the long awaited statement on status of the latest comet mining operation:-

'...despite all the problems with CPC's resource scheduling program, we managed to retrieve the vital ingredient of life just in the nick of time. Optimally, we would have recovered twelve hundred tons, but in the circumstances we got just over eight hundred and forty tons net. Given the low rate of seepage, we will be fully covered for the best part of a decade. And I am very delighted to say folks, our flamingo populations that had become temporarily disoriented, can once again happily resume their place in the Wildlife Preserve.' He said cheerily at the conclusion of his broadcast over the six o'clock TV news program.

There was a euphoric moment of cheer by people right across the ship. Their world had come perilously close to suffering a major drought. Thanks to the pioneering efforts of Zakarov et al, the *Centauri Princess* was once again sailing merrily on her lonely voyage across the dark of the vast cosmic emptiness that stretched to near-eternity in all directions. Should the unthinkable have happened here, there could have been no outside help from anywhere within the sphere of human reach. Every man, woman and child of eligible age sailing on this lonely ark ship - now over a trillion miles out and two thousand years from Earth - was once again made to be intimately aware of this chilling fact.

That evening, the various religious communities held services of thankfulness, in accordance to their own individual customs. Mosques, synagogues, churches and other places of worship right across Utopia were having trouble fitting in the unexpectedly large crowds that turned up. Their prayers were filled with expressions of appreciation to the gods for the success of the latest mining operation. Muslims of course faced in the direction of Makkah - marked out by the so-called 'qiblah' as referred to in Arabic. From the *Centauri Princess'* present interstellar location, that focal point of all prayers in the Islamic faith was precisely in the direction of our distant Sun, now appearing as only a bright yellow star in the starship's rear view mirror. The milli-arcsecond diameter, insignificant flicker of light that was supposed to be planet Earth, was never separately discernible to anyone peering in that direction; from this distance it was invisible to the unaided eye, and always lost somewhere within the overwhelming brilliance of our Sun's own fiery glow. In fact, the angular width of our entire solar system - from Mercury to Pluto - was less than the width of a full moon as seen in the night skies of Earth; a person holding out their thumb at arms length would have been able to cover it up quite easily.

A further insight, perhaps worthy of note here, is that

no cult or religion exclusively devoted to 'sun worship' here on Earth would have been justified in performing such a ritual beyond this point on the outbound interstellar voyage. Sun worshipping religions are based on a fundamental pillar of faith which upholds the Sun as the most supreme source of all light and heat to their followers. As the *Centauri Princess* was presently crossing the *'Ahad radius'* - an imaginary boundary that marked the edge of Sun's light domination - from here onwards, the universe's total background glow would outshine the feeble amounts of light and heat coming from our own distant Sun. Thus, *the Sun would no longer be the most supreme source of overall light and heat* to a sun worshipper, invalidating his/her core pillar of faith…

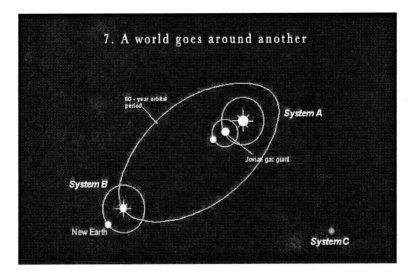

7. A world goes around another

Karim Yurchenko was regarded, at best as a very wise old man and, at worst, an eccentric old recluse. For as long as anyone could remember, he had lived all by himself in an old fashioned, shabby-looking house on the edge of the Black Forest in the Lower Province. His place had the classic look of something really old; exterior walls looked like the nesting place of birds and small forest animals that burrowed their way in.

As a result of his complete isolation from the rest of the starship communities, he had developed many abilities as a mystic and a medium over the seventy three years of his life. His senses were attuned to the inaudible whispers from unseen speakers; his mind reaching beyond the occult. He knew many untold secrets about the spiritual aspects of this voyage, that virtually no one on the ship could ever have been aware of.

Presently, he stood on the area of open ground in front of his house in the evening darkness, listening to the chirping of crickets in the Black Forest that surrounded him. He wore a cowboy-style black hat that partially covered his long, grey hair that flowed past shoulder length. He looked up at the night sky and saw tiny clusters of lights that marked settlements across to the *Princess'* opposite side. They appeared to shine with a flickering rhythm, much like how camp fires burn on distant hillsides after nightfall.

'May god have mercy on the souls of those who are visited by the beasts tonight,' he said softly to himself.

He went back inside the house and sat in the eerie atmosphere of a small, candle lit room. Shadows of artefacts danced all around him, as the candle's flame wavered in the warm breeze flowing through the house. He closed his eyes, and gradually descended into a session of meditation.

As his mind crossed the borderline into a mode of hallucination, the creatures came vividly to life. In his self-induced confrontation, Yurchenko was receiving clear messages of communication from the beasts. In his mind's eye, the leader of the pack of wolf angels beckoned to him with its claws. Next thing, before he knew it, he could see himself flying off with them, as if he too possessed the same kind of mysterious power that they did.

He was travelling ever faster, across the vast expanse of inky blackness that separated the stars. He sensed that he was being taken to their world, wherever that might be. The stars of the surrounding cosmic night sky in this close to light-speed trek, were warped into a circular window that condensed into a ball of light in front of him. It glowed in a colourful display, as receding stars appeared red whilst approaching ones appeared blue, in the doppler shift. This compression of the universe's starlight into a ball was to be expected of course, from the relativistic squeeze predicted by Einstein's Special Theory of Relativity. Yurchenko continued trailing behind the beasts in their phantom flight, ever faster, drawing closer toward the speed of light.

Then, suddenly, he felt things were starting to slow down again. The relativistic effects on the cosmic night sky appeared to be playing back in a reverse order from that which he had experienced when he was accelerating. He had arrived at *their* world, wherever that was, he thought. Then, materialising before him as he watched, Yurchenko saw a tantalising cosmic display that he felt certain no human mind could ever have even imagined before. He instantly recognised the Alpha Centauri system shown in its full glory, with its three suns glowing in their contrasting colours in the distance. The system looked veiled and mysterious. The whole scene appeared to be shrouded in a wispy cloud of interstellar gas and dust that was backlit by the three suns, causing it to glow in a myriad of subtle shades and colours. And he realised that he had, somehow, crossed a near-50,000 year journey separating the starship from that system, in a matter of only a few minutes...Such an astonishing feat could only have been achieved through some mysterious, inter-dimensional 'worm holing' that evaded the normal intertwining of space and time, effectively bypassing the physical light years.

The wolf angels glided effortlessly through a belt of far orbiting asteroids, marking the outer edges of Alpha Centauri's shores, in their phantom flight. The triple star system loomed large ahead in Yurchenko's present dream state. The brightest of the three stars was yellow (like our own Sol) the next brightest one was orange in colour. Finally, Proxima Centauri, the smallest of the three, was depicted as a deep reddish glow. As the system drew closer, New Earth was there, shining as a thin crescent close to its orange sun of Alpha Centauri B. Then the Jupiter sized gas giant, orbiting Alpha Centauri A, emerged from behind its yellow sun.

That was when he saw another world - hitherto unknown to him or anyone else on the ship. That could only be a giant moon circling the Jupiter sized gas giant, he thought. It was to where the wolf angels appeared to be taking him. As he neared the yellow sun of Alpha Centauri A, their world loomed large in the sky ahead of him, as the beasts descended down past its cloud tops, toward the surface.

At that point, the lead creature turned around in mid-flight to present its evil face toward Yurchenko. It made a series of wild gestures, as if it were trying to communicate with him. And then the creature spoke out loudly in a half human, half wolf-like growl:

'Go back. You will not be welcome here! You will not be welcome here! You will not be welcome here!...'

The phantom beast repeated this message, sounding like a fading echo, as it disappeared from view, gradually becoming immersed into the engulfing clouds of its home planet.

Yurchenko's consciousness was suddenly thrown back into his physical body, as he awoke from his self-induced hallucination. The memories of his virtual trip to the wolf angels' home planet, in his dream state, remained every bit as vivid as if he had physically been there.

The Deep Space Telescope Facility (DSTF) was a small building located on the outer edge of the ship, toward the front nose cone of its twelve mile long, bullet-shaped outline, three miles outside the main biosphere. In a view of the *Centauri Princess* seen from the outside looking in, the location of the DSTF was reminiscent of the cockpit of a jumbo jet here on Earth. Due to its unique location close to the central spin axis of the starship, the small habitat of the DSTF experienced only a tiny amount of artificial gravity from the ship's spin. All personnel who were working there or visiting, needed to have special zero-g training and obtain formal clearance from the MMC in advance. They also needed to wear shoes with magnetic soles that gripped onto the nickel-iron floor of the facility, to help cope with the effects of virtually total weightlessness. The lower gravity here of course arose from the differential angular accelerations as a result of circular motion.

The easiest way to visualise this under normal gravity here on Earth would be as follows. Take an empty cup, say a plastic or polystyrene coffee cup, and half fill it with water. Now if you hold the cup in your hand and simply turn it upside down, it's no surprise that the water just spills out. If you thread a long piece of plastic wire or tough string through two holes bored on opposite sides around the rim of the cup and whirl it around at head-height, the water will not spill out, since it will be constantly pushing outward towards the bottom of the cup under centrifugal forces. Now, if you significantly shorten the length of the wire or piece of string and repeat the experiment, whirling the cup at the same speed as before, the chances are the water will now spill out; for a shorter string, you will need to significantly increase the rate at which you whirl the cup to ensure the same amount of centrifugal force is at work to keep the water inside the cup. Similarly, since the DSTF is located on a smaller radius vector away from the central spin-axis of the ship, it experiences significantly different centrifugal forces compared to the outer rim, which is of course rotating at just the right speed in order to generate one-g of Earth gravity equivalent for the *Centauri Princess'* biosphere/crew hab. The spin rate of the ship as a whole hardly ever varied through the mission, since there was no external tidal forces or other influences to act as any kind of drag in the interstellar vacuum. Nevertheless, the starship design did incorporate spin thrusters as contingency, to meet any potential needs for readjustment.

The starship's four fully steerable optical telescopes, each one located at ninety degree intervals around the outer body and looking out into the surrounding universe, served as the 'eyes' of the DSTF. Collectively, they acted as a wide-baseline interferometry set up for greater resolving power, when observing objects in the forward path of the ship. Processing of the images that they produced and their overall steering, coordination and management, were all handled from the DSTF.

Dermot Azura was the director of interstellar navigation and astronomy. Him and his small team of four, worked inside the DSTF in complete isolation from the main communities across the interior. Theirs was a specialist function that involved staying over at the facility on a temporary basis, akin to how astronauts spend time in isolation inside the zero-g environment of a space station, such as the International Space Station operating in present day low Earth orbit.

In addition to its routine use for astronomy, the DSTF also served a critical function in long range navigation. As the starship drifted silently in the dark waters of an endless interstellar ocean, whose shores reached out to near eternity in every direction one cared to look, precise navigation was a major challenge. With no magnetic fields, no bright planets and no global positioning systems for relative referencing, triangulation by the minute positional shifts of nearby stars in the surrounding cosmic night sky, as the ship edged forward, was the only means of gauging how far it had travelled between Sol and Alpha Centauri at any given instant.

However, accurate positional fixes were required only once or twice during each generation, since the ark ship only crawled at snail's pace compared to other, faster means of interstellar propulsion. With a total mass of the *Centauri Princess* approaching a colossal two hundred trillion kilograms, its nuclear powered engines pushed it forward at an average speed of sixty thousand miles per hour (one and a half times the speeds of NASA's *Voyagers 1* and *2*, that are presently heading out towards the stars). At that rate, it narrowed the gulf separating our solar system from Alpha Centauri at the minute rate of just two per cent every one thousand years…

Azura and Zakarov were old friends. Their acquaintance went back all the way to the days when they both graduated with first class honours degrees from the Technology Innovations Center, in the starship's educational complex. Zakarov had made the special trip to the DSTF using the starship's underground, extended elevator network. Azura was very glad to see him, as the two men greeted each other with warm handshakes.

'I just wanted to say, I think you did an excellent job in the latest mining operation. For a minute back there, you people in the control room had quite a few of us worried,' Azura complimented.

'You know how we are,' Zakarov said, with a hint of smile brought to his otherwise cold face.

Azura was regarded by everyone within his sphere of contact as something of an intellectual boffin. He was of the same age as Zakarov, had a medium build with a thin face. The thick-lensed spectacles he wore added to his looks of a pure academic. As if it were needed, the giant poster of Albert Einstein laced across the far side wall of the DSTF's control room, brought home Azura's passionate strive for 'geniusness' in all that he did.

'About these nightmares, Crista and Chang have come up with this idiosyncratic notion that the creatures are somehow emanating from a planet in the Alpha Centauri system. If that were to be true, the thing we need to establish is do they emanate from New Earth, our destination planet, or another one that we have simply yet to discover?' Zakarov said.

'Well, that is interesting. Although I find these speculations rather absurd, to say the least.' Azura didn't like the gist of what he was hearing. 'Over the past few decades, we have been closely studying the seasonal changes on New Earth. Spectroscopic signatures of the kind of life prevalent on its surface have said very little that would set it apart from our ancestors' home planet of Earth.'

As Zakarov and Azura stood talking in the DSTF's main control room, through its glazed outer wall, they momentarily caught a glimpse of the famous constellation of Crux — the 'Southern Cross' — shining brilliantly in the black sky ahead of the ship. As the vessel gently rotated about its spin axis, the constellation's colourful stars glided across the giant window; an ever changing cosmic slide show that played back perpetually. Alpha Centauri, in the neighbouring constellation of Centaurus, was not on view directly from the DSTF, since it was hidden behind the nose cone of the ship itself, that constantly pointed in its direction.

A tall, slender woman in her early thirties entered the control room, taking slow steps as she walked under the prevailing conditions of zero-g. She laid out a tray with refreshments.

'Please help yourselves to some warm coffee and biscuits,' she said.

Azura turned around, slightly startled.

'Oh, thank you Gina,' he said as she was about to leave the control room.

The two men continued their discussions, sipping coffee out of zero-g cups through special straws that catered for containment of the liquid under the abnormal conditions.

'What about an all-telescope, wide baseline

interferometry scan of the region around Alpha Centauri A with the faint object camera? Has that been done lately?' Zakarov enquired.

'We simply have not had the resources to extend our studies to star A, other than what we have known all along - that it has a gas giant, about the size of Jupiter, sitting bang in the middle of its life zone. Around one point two astronomical units out in terms of orbital distance.'

Azura continued, 'Besides, even if the wolf angels did manage to thrive on such a gaseous world somehow, what is the rationale for them to then leap out across these enormous light years and haunt us in our dreams?' He laughed out loudly. 'Have those two suddenly become 'spiritual' or something? What the hell has happened to their scientific logic?'

'Wild speculations,' Zakarov agreed. The DSTF's control room was momentarily thrown into a silence, as he thought long and hard.

At last Zakarov said, 'How about a large moon orbiting that Jupiter sized gas giant? Hypothetically speaking if such a planet were to exist, then there is nothing to rule out the possibility of it harbouring some exotic variety of alien life that might *just* have some extraordinary psychic ability to roam between solar systems. Also, we must remember that Alpha Centauri is significantly older than Sol, so any potential life forms in that system would likely be way ahead of us in the evolutionary race anyway. There's no harm in speculating, is there?'

Azura smiled and shook his head in gentle disagreement.

Zakarov was all too well aware of Azura's hard, scientific shell that would be difficult to penetrate with 'outside the box' speculations that went a bit further than the accepted norm. He now had full confirmation of that trait in the man.

He looked at his wristcom.

'Well Dermot, thanks for your time but I really must get going.'

'You people are always too busy in that control room, nowadays,' Azura said.

He saw Zakarov out towards the elevator.

'You must come along to the Launch Day ball,' Zakarov invited.

'Gosh, doesn't the year go by just like a flash? I will try.'

'And please have the lovely Mrs. Azura accompany you for once. I look forward to seeing you both there.'

Zakarov was of course referring to the annual Launch Day celebrations; a convention that had been followed ever since the first 'day' when the starship departed from Earth. That was officially designated as the moment when the very last space shuttle, carrying the last of the initial nine hundred colony crew, had boarded the ship in high Earth orbit, and the entrance was officially sealed. That instant fell on July 30th, 2275 AD. On that day, each year, celebrations would be held in a hi-tec entertainment hall in central Utopia, to mark the anniversary of humanity's first, one-way interstellar departure from the cradle of planet Earth.

'I'll get my people to do some detailed studies of the life zone around Alpha Centauri A. We'll keep you posted,' Azura assured. 'Oh, and Zakarov, one more thing. At the next Systems Meeting of the MMC, can you please raise a request for upgrading some of the DSTF's hardware we talked about earlier? Instrument sensitivity is crucial if we are to gain good results from our scan.'

'Will try. You know what the Committee is like on, what it classes as 'non-critical' systems,' Zakarov said, as the elevator doors closed in front of him.

The DSTF, and indeed much of the robotics and hardware technologies on the ship, were of a similar standard to that when the vessel was first built and launched from Earth orbit. New hardware that could be used to boost the technological capabilities of the starship's society was expected to be scarce along the voyage. In-flight comet mining merely provided water for topping up life support reserves and chemical fuels for auxiliary propulsion. Consumable items, so to speak.

When it came to extracting metallic ores and other raw materials, the starship communities relied upon chance encounters with significant sized planetoids - miniature planetary bodies in their own right. So far into the voyage, the distribution of such bodies had proved sparse across the inner belt of the solar Oort cloud. Once encountered in the forward path of the ship, their successful mining meant killing all ship velocity to zero and docking into a closed orbit around the planetoid for anywhere between one and several years, at a stretch. Shuttle craft would then be despatched from the ship down to the planetoid's surface, with engineering teams and robots establishing a temporary mining base there. They would then employ whatever technology was deemed necessary to physically carry out the mining process, and use the shuttle fleet to ferry material back up to the *Centauri Princess*. Given the gigantic scale of the ship and the priceless amounts of forward momentum that would be lost in any planetoid encounters, the mission would realistically only make such a rendezvous in the extremes of some kind of an emergency, as opposed to just routine hardware replenishment.

One possible way around outright orbital encounters with planetoids would have been to manufacture and launch a small mining ship at a faster speed, using the starship's own sixty thousand miles per hour speed as a base platform. The small mining ship would then rendezvous with the planetoid at a great distance ahead of the main mission, carry out the hardware mining and return back to the mother ship as it flew past. That was, after all, how the un-manned Alpha, Beta, Gamma,...nav platforms operated. The issue with this approach was primarily one of crew safety : unlike with the fully autonomous comet-mining nav platforms, the planetoid-mining small ship would need to be a *manned* undertaking, carrying a fully-fledged team of engineers and exposing them to great speeds through the interstellar dark, with unseen micrometeoroid and whatever other health hazards that awaited them up ahead. Thus, planetoid mining was both a 'risky' and 'costly' business to say the least, and needed to be carefully handled in the light of whatever emergency prevailed onboard the *Centauri Princess* at the time. If the fuel losses during the initial slow down and subsequent speed up could be more than offset by the hardware resources gained out of the encounter, then the economic justification was there for mining a planetoid, irrespective of whether or not there was an 'emergency' as such.

As it so happened, over the past two thousand years the starship communities had mined only one such mini-world, to partly replenish their hardware and raw material needs. That orbital encounter was not entirely for 'emergency' reasons, but rather as a feasibility exercise relatively early on in the mission, so as to prove that future requirements along the eye-watering 50,000 years of darkness that still lay ahead, could be managed in a similar way. As an incidental, surprise element to that raw materials mining task, the starship communities had also managed to unearth a commodity that would have been unquantifiably valuable by monetary standards back here on Earth: *they came across the largest diamond find ever.* The giant stone had been discovered buried, some two thousand feet underneath the icy crustal regolith. However, following its successful mining, the lucky folk enjoying the adventures of the mission at that time had a hard time seeing any serious use for the vast amounts of this treasure. Once all the jewellery stores across the interior had been filled with diamond necklaces, diamond watches, diamond rings, diamond wristcoms…the remainder was used to build a few landmarks in and around Utopia, to symbolise their epic find to subsequent generations.

Given the scarce distribution of hardware-rich planetoids within the Oort cloud, emphasis for ongoing technology evolution onboard the ship leaned more toward preserving and maintaining what was already there and much less on expansion and new innovations. Having said that though, there were many new advances in the *software* capabilities. One example of this was in the artificial intelligence advances of the repairbot fleet. At the time of departure from Earth, they could barely roll along on uneven ground or have comprehensive speech capabilities when it came to interacting freely with humans. Besides, their only function was to repair things —hence the name 'repairbot'. Now, two thousand years into the voyage, they could fly around autonomously across the vast, cylindrical interior from floor to ceiling, and carry out virtually every manually intensive task with the minimum of human supervision. In addition, they could act as pet robots for young children and serve as shopping assistants for the elderly and the infirm.

Another major area of both hardware and software enhancement was with the suite of Alpha, Beta, Gamma, etc. platforms. A total of anywhere between ten and fifteen such navigation platforms were continually operating ahead of the mission. Once launched from the ship, they could now identify upcoming resource islands and autonomously mine them with far less guidance from the control room, thanks to CPC's vastly improved software capabilities. They were now effectively serving as a remote extension of 'limbs and senses' of the ship, up to some half a trillion miles in front. The promise was very much there that one day, in the not too distant future, the *Centauri Princess* would become totally self-managing in executing all of its inflight resourcing needs for water and biosphere life support.

Caroline Polansky lived all by herself in a suburban street on the outskirts of Utopia, not far from the famous *diamond bridge* over Eridanus. In its basic design, the *diamond bridge* was merely a suspension style of river bridge which routed road transport over Eridanus as it flowed between central Utopia and all the way out into the broader interior.

As its name implied, the distinctive feature of this bridge was that its entire framework had been built up from pure, sparkling clear, highest quality diamond! It was constructed toward the end of the first millennium, following the discovery of an enormous sized natural diamond (as mentioned earlier), found buried deep beneath the surface ice of a planetoid. The stone had then been polished and cut using lasers into parts suitable to build the long bridge, along with a few other less well known features in and around Utopia. Given the high refractive index of polished diamond, the bridge was the most distinctive feature in the whole of Utopia. When directly in view from other parts of the starship's cylindrical interior, it could be easily seen as a fiery landmark, blazing with lustre during the day.

Having a home close to the *diamond bridge* added somewhat to Caroline's already sparkling profile. She was fairly well known right across the interior, as a woman of majestic beauty and elegance, who was also caring and level headed in nature at the same time. She put her caring attributes to good use, in her career as a nurse at the Medical Facility.

In common with all the other homes on Inertia Drive and in that part of town generally, Caroline's house was built from quality western red cedar for much of its construction. It had a shingled roof and three bedrooms on the first floor. It was set well back from the main street, with a long driveway that was paved in grey concrete, running across a somewhat parched, lawn. A Douglas fir stood at the centre of the front yard, giving a shaded outlook to the residence.

Presently Caroline was in the shower, freshening up ready to go out for the evening. She'd arranged to see a movie at the multi-screen in Utopia with Alcyone. The shower cubicle was incorporated within a bathroom suite of tiled walls and white fixtures. Fragrances from scented soaps and hair care products hung in the steamy air. As the lukewarm water sprayed into her hair, sensuously caressing her scalp, Caroline's thoughts drifted back to her ex-lover. A part of her still wished…if only things had been a little different. But it wasn't meant to be, and she always believed things happened for a reason. Always. If only she knew what those reasons were for *this* situation? The odds of a relationship working out after three months of intimacy, was quoted as just one in five. Those were pretty firm figures, based on the latest surveys she'd read about in the *Centauri Life* magazine.

She turned off the water, towelled herself dry and walked across into the first floor bedroom. Since breaking up with Sharuk she was getting used to being alone in the house again, although she did miss the company, especially at night. At the height of their relationship, he would normally stay over during the week and they would have a break at weekends. Now, that was a thing of the past and the house always felt empty—and silent. Except for music and entertainment, that she selectively put on the screen to escape the loneliness.

Looking through the closet, Caroline pondered what she ought to put on for evening wear. It was warm out there, with the air standing thick and motionless. Subtropical June nights always made her sweat, so she went for light clothing. Just then the soft, musical chimes from the door bell sounded. She looked across to the bedroom's wall-embedded interactive screen. It showed a camera view looking out into the front yard. Alcyone was there, waiting.

'Won't be more than a few minutes,' Caroline shouted; her voice reaching her friend via the screen's interactive features.

She got dressed, put on some light make up and remembered to shut all the windows on the first floor, front and back, via a control menu on the interactive screen. Closing the windows and drawing the curtains was an instinctive thing to do before going out for the evening. Not that there was any risk of burglary of course, with CPC's security systems active around the clock. Even though Caroline was someone who never leaned much toward supernatural beliefs, her instincts probably had roots that delved deeper in that direction. In the legends, fairy tales and popular myths that lay buried in the miniature world's antiquity, trees were associated with evil spirits. The suburban forests in and around Utopia, as beautiful as they were during the day, could turn cruel after nightfall. The mind of an isolated young woman living all by herself, was susceptible to turn the night breezes blowing in from ancient woodlands into something more sinister, under the right conditions.

She sprayed on some perfume and put on her wristcom in a hurry, before leaving the house.

'You're never gonna guess who that creep is with now,' Alcyone said, as they walked on.

'You mean you know? Who?' Caroline asked in disbelief, glancing toward her friend.

'I saw them kissing inside his Corvette the other day. And maybe a little more.'

'Do you just mind telling me who she is please?'

Alcyone paused briefly, to deliberately prolong the suspense.

'Of all people, Zayna—the control room's Miss Vanity,' she said at last.

'Bitch!' Caroline said. Her face told Alcyone just how astonished she was, but underneath she kept calm. 'I wish her all the luck though. Have you told anyone else?'

'Yeah, your uncle. That was another nail in Sharuk's coffin and Zakarov now has legal grounds for displacing that creep from the control room for sure!'

They walked on towards the multi-screen in the west end of Utopia, as the evening grew dark around them.

The movie theatre was dimly lit and atmospheric inside. On this occasion, it looked unusually quiet ahead of the major screening. Its audience was no more than a handful of people, who sat in isolated spots scattered across the large hall. The faint spotlighting cast a decidedly reddish glow onto the mostly empty black leather seats, that were arranged in adjacent rows. Colour of the theatre lighting had been purposely designed to enhance the mood of the movie - which was a romantic comedy set on the Red Planet, back in the early twenty third century.

Caroline and Alcyone sat at the back, close to a young couple in an adjacent row.

'This should be fun,' Alcyone said with excitement, as the show started.

'I hope so.' Caroline replied, munching popcorn.

For the next hour or so, they watched the story plot unfold on the holographically projected, virtual 3D screen. Occasionally, there was the odd moment of amusement from the show's comedy aspects, when the small crowd laughed out loud. Apart from those, there was mainly off-screen silence inside the dark theatre.

Toward the second half of the movie, the pacing proved to be really slow and the characters were not quite as strong as what the trailers had made out. Alcyone was enjoying it a lot more than Caroline though, who looked and felt rather sleepy.

'I need to go to the bathroom. Can you tell me what happens?' Alcyone said, getting up from her seat.

'I'll try - if I don't nod off, that is.'

Caroline pinched herself to stay awake. The hero on the screen was onboard an Elysium Express passenger train, on his way to meet his would-be sweet heart in a city located out in the red Martian deserts. The train finally reached the desert city, which was presently shrouded in a major dust storm, that made a howling sound on the screen. His date was there to greet him, in midst of the large crowd waiting at the railway station. Strangely enough, her appearance and features were rather similar to Caroline's own, and she wore a pink hat and a similar coloured velvety dress for the occasion.

No matter how hard she tried, Caroline's eyes just kept closing…The cinema screen gradually started to go blurred, as if someone were defocusing the movie projector. The images became murky and faint. The sounds of the dust storm faded, and eventually there was only silence. She was on the edge of sleep. Then she felt herself to be somehow on the theatre screen itself, *as if she were starring in the movie, too.* In her dream state, Caroline was the one waiting on the platform. She was waiting to meet her date arriving on the Elysium Express train.

The dust storm continued to rage violently outside, throwing up red sands into the pink Martian sky. Caroline looked out through the station's glazed walls, out into the surrounding deserts of Elysium Planitia. A tornado had formed out of the gathering whirlwind and the red landscape in the background gradually lost its sharp definition. The storm rapidly marched in toward the station, threatening to deliver a devastating blow. The crowd on the platform was braced for the imminent strike. As she watched in horror, the spectre of the tornado gradually faded into blackness again, as the phantom movie became due for another scene change...

But then she realised she was falling down what appeared to be a dark, bottomless tunnel. On Mars?...on the *Centauri Princess*?...or somewhere else? Caroline had lost all bearings as to her whereabouts in this alternate reality, as her nightmare deepened further. The tunnel looked narrow, much like a well and to be of incalculable depth. It became deeper and darker as she fell. She kept on falling through it, faster and faster.

Eventually, her rate of free fall seemed to be slowing. That was when she saw the illusive wolf angels waiting at the other end, at what must have been the tunnel's very bottom, she sensed. The archangel leader snarled at her, exposing its gruesome white teeth and flapping its vast, semi-transparent wings. It had deeply set, glowing red eyes and enormous fangs. A cloud of grey mist vented from its nostrils, as it leapt up menacingly, to try and catch hold of her feet. She felt herself to be motionless, hovering inside the dark tunnel, within several yards of its bottom. The pitch blackness pressed against her body from all directions. The archangel growled again, glaring up at her from below with savage eyes. It made the most horrific sounds imaginable, that echoed up through the black tunnel…

'Wake up, Caroline -' Alcyone shouted, nudging her. 'The movie's nearly over, you've gotta see the ending.'

Caroline was shaking with fear and gasped, as she awoke from her brief nightmare. Her face glistened in the dim theatre illumination, with sweat ruining her light make up.

'They were there,' she said, pointing toward the screen.

'You mean you had the nightmare?'

She nodded. 'How long was I gone for?'

'Gosh, I only left you for about ten minutes.' Alcyone said.

'Als, I wanna go home asap. Can I ask a huge favour from you please?'

'Sure, ask away.'

'Do you mind staying over at my place tonight?'

'I'll have to let Joey know. You must have been pretty deeply in there, by the looks of things.'

'I was, and it was absolutely hell,' Caroline said, still trembling from the experience.

When it came to law enforcement, the MMC maintained a small force of police officers who patrolled the streets of Utopia, mainly at night. Crime levels were generally very low, and peaked in the juvenile category with young offenders occasionally causing mischievous deeds, like fighting and truenting from school. Law and order were enforced in the same way as in a small state back here on Earth. A panel of MMC appointed judges exercised judicial duties in conformance to the starship's robust, computer guarded, computer enforced, statute books. The legal frameworks that governed the balance of justice across the miniature world were essentially as old as the voyage itself; they had been carefully formulated and written under the ruling sovereignty of the first president, Joseph Lexington, and no flexibility had been built into CPC for any further alteration, ever since.

In terms of guarding the vast acres of pine forests, lakes and open prairies across the interior, there were autonomous surveillance and monitoring devices in operation - much like CCTVs in use here on Earth today. They were generally kept concealed from public view and were remotely networked to CPC's central monitoring system. Thus, the entire six hundred square kilometres of the interior surface area of the ship could be watched, virtually down to the last square inch, on a continuous basis.

Critics of the scheme had originally found it to be too dictatorial and akin to a 'military ship'. However, long term behavioural models developed from many decades of experience with closed societies on Earth, on the Moon and on Mars, had shown that the only way to prevent any factionalisation and their long term collapse, was to adopt a fairly rigid system, such as the one successfully operated here. The authority that oversaw the surveillance system was the MMC, and that was democratically elected by the people. So the starship communities, ultimately, had some element of human intervention in the process, and the system took full account of the human dimension as opposed to just being 'cold and robotic'.

The starship's court house was a distinctive looking, elegant building situated at the heart of Utopia, adjacent to MMC headquarters. It had all the hallmarks associated with a twenty first century public building of stature back here on Earth, complete with Corinthian pillars, large wooden doors and a domed roof.

On this occasion, Zakarov had arranged a hearing to decide what action needs to be taken against Sharuk on account of his misconduct over the past several weeks. He had been summoned to the court house at short notice, on the severity of the case that had mounted up against him.

The chief justice was wearing a traditional style wig as he sat on the throne of the judiciary panel, flanked by two of his senior council members who were seated on either side. Inside the chamber room were also present Nikolaus Zakarov and the starship president, Zed Lincoln, Sharuk Rashid himself and his advising attorney. A small crowd, consisting of members of the ordinary public, were also present as drop-in guests, who came to watch the trial.

With the court session having been in progress for a

while, the head of the judiciary panel was speaking out in a loud, authoritative tone.

'You are being removed from further duty in the control room as chief navigation officer, on account of the charges brought against you. Namely, maliciously and wilfully tampering with the resource scheduling module of CPC and, contrary to regulations, engaging in a relationship with a closely working colleague. The former charge is unquestionably the more graver of the two, as it put the entire mission into jeopardy. How do you plead?'

Sharuk stood up with glaring eyes, and a brick-red face. Sweat poured from his forehead, and he looked as if his blood were boiling in his veins.

'And just where is the evidence for all of this?' He said, in a poisonous voice.

The advising attorney, sitting besides him, tugged on the end of his jacket sleeve, urging him to remain calm.

'A member of the inquiry panel will be happy to take you through the details behind how you skilfully misaligned CPC's base variables, after which you thought you would cover your tracks by altering the document editing dates. Correct?'

There was a brief silence.

One of the council members sitting besides the chief justice, took over. He spoke in a stern, judicial tone.

'You see Mr. Rashid, contrary to popular belief, there are avenues for us to gain access to CPC's innermost workings under certain, exceptional circumstances. An inquiry panel has spent the past few weeks unravelling the great mysteries behind the resource scheduling module's sudden failures to issue a level one alert ahead of our encounter with Comet C dash 336. The panel went through the binary encoding procedures that underlie CPC's clock function to uncover every last detail of your tinkerings. It had to be done manually - bit by bit - and cost the panel valuable time. In the end, your malicious acts were unravelled from the chip level information.'

The judge sipped some water, creating a momentary silence inside the courtroom.

He continued with the same stern, authoritative tone.

'The Mission Management Committee had placed great trust in you by giving you complete autonomy to manage the most critical, most fundamental pillars of this mission, and you chose to breach that trust. You are a most evil man, Mr Rashid. So we ask you again. How do you plead?'

After a long silence, Sharuk finally pleaded guilty, as he was cornered by the weight of evidence overwhelmingly in favour of Zakarov. He was to be removed from the control room with immediate effect and Zayna and Joey were to cover Sharuk's role in addition to their normal duties, pending the recruitment of a suitable replacement. In the meantime, Zakarov was to take full command of the Navigation and Control Complex as an enlargement to his existing, varied roles across the ship.

'This court will in due course advise you of your new line of duty. In the meantime, you are being placed into a probationary status, and your every move will be closely monitored for the next three months. Case dismissed.'

The judiciary panel concluded Sharuk's trial, with that notice served on him. The rapid and targeted conclusion of this particular case is testimony to how the MMC would bear down like a mountain of bricks on the few and far between individuals who occasionally dared to step out of line.

There followed a roar of conversations that echoed across the large chamber room of the court house.

'Congratulations on your secondment, Zakarov. I wish you well,' said Zed Lincoln.

'Thank you mister president. I was hoping for promotion under much better circumstances though,' Zakarov replied modestly, with a smile.

'I am sure you will do well.'

With Sharuk's downfall, Lincoln automatically favoured Zakarov to be the new successor to the control room's command, even though one or two others had been in line. This was of course due to a subtle political undercurrent that ran through the MMC hierarchy over successive generations. Zakarov's mother, when she was alive, was a first cousin to Lincoln's father, who had successfully ruled the *Centauri Princess* as president over the two prior generations that preceded Lincoln's presidency. Thus, whilst members of the MMC were superficially seen to be elected through a democratic voting system, the presidents were kept within the dynasty that Joseph Lexington had originally started on initial departure from Earth, all those centuries earlier. Therefore, in essence, the apex of the miniature world's chain of command was akin to an autocratically ruling monarchy system of a small state here on Earth.

A tropical thunder storm was brewing in the dark skies above Yurchenko's house, as he sat on the veranda reading a book. He heard the distinctive hooting sounds of moiurs in the forests nearby as they became restless, sensing the sudden weather change. Winds started to pick up in speed and they howled across the surrounding expanse of the Black Forest, with trees swaying over his shabby-looking house. In the midst of these sounds, he could faintly hear the engine of an approaching rover.

Zakarov parked Betty in the forest clearing in the distance and hurried over towards Yurchenko's house, ahead of the downpour.

'Howdy. It's turning quite mean out there,' he said.

'Who the devil are you?' Yurchenko wasn't used to receiving that many strangers.

'Zakarov. Nikolaus Zakarov, I'm in command of the Navigation and Control Complex over in Utopia.' He asserted with a tone of authority. 'Make it a practice of not keeping a wristcom? I had no way of reaching you. I need your help in pinning down the home planet of these god damn wolf angels. Mind if I come in?'

It was starting to rain, with big drops gliding down onto the shingled roof of Yurchenko's house and drenching its west-facing walls, as they 'curved in' from up above.

'Thought I told everything I know to Joey.'

Zakarov took shelter from the storm and sat on an elegantly crafted rosewood bench next to Yurchenko, on the veranda. He sensed a strong whiff of incense coming from inside the house, which the mystic must be using in his nightly rituals, Zakarov thought.

'There are some secrets which you've been keeping all to yourself, old guy. Do you realise what's going on up there each and every single night?' He asked in a serious tone and pointed up, as he referred to the residents of Utopia across to the other side of the curved interior.

'Phantom beasts. Creatures of pure energy. Claws, fangs, wings. They come,' Yurchenko said, as if reading out a poem from the book in his hand.

He closed the bluish-white textbook, and laid it down on the floor besides him.

'Listen to me old guy, I didn't come here all this way to hear you talk in riddles. I want to know *exactly* what these things are and where they come from.'

'What they are is dependent on the phase of encounter. Where they come from is the planet around a planet.'

Yurchenko's words just did not make any sense.

'Look, I was physically bruised by one of these things the other night,' Zakarov said, pointing to the scar on his right shoulder.

A huge rumble of thunder sounded overhead, as it shook the wooden house with vibrations. The rain started to turn into more of a torrential downpour, with CPC significantly dimming the light levels from local miniature suns so as to mimic overcast skies, as seen during a natural thunder storm here on Earth.

'The planes merged in your encounter. You were unfortunate.'

'You're not making a lot of sense old guy. If you want to earn a few E-Ms for this consultation, I would encourage you to adopt a more expressive style of communication. What 'planes' are you talking about?'

The grey haired man closed his eyes. His thinking was stifled by images and shadows that made fleeting appearances in his mind's eye.

'They exist in an alternate dimension. A different plane from ours. Occasionally, the two planes intersect. If one happens to have a nightmare at that instant, then the beasts can cause physical harm.' He spoke like someone undergoing hypnosis. 'They are angelic. But angels of satan, not of god. Dark, and of evil intent.'

Yurchenko opened his pale blue eyes again, coming out of the meditative trance.

The rain poured down harder, with more thunder and lightning flashes causing the sky to sparkle over the Black Forest, as the two men watched.

'You said something about 'a planet around a planet'. Is that where they come from?' Zakarov asked.

'Their world circles a larger world. It circles the yellow sun. The yellow sun of Alpha Centauri A.'

'They were right,' Zakarov said softly, referring to the hypothesis that Crista and Chang had formulated. 'Are you certain those darn things *do not* come from New Earth itself - our destination?'

'In my inquiries, they only warned me not to go to their world,' Yurchenko said.

'The wolf angels see us as a threat to their planet?'

'Yes. I think so.'

That would explain the relentlessness with which they had been making appearances, Zakarov thought.

Since the *Centauri Princess'* course line was headed generally toward Alpha Centauri, it was impossible for the wolf angels, or any outside party for that matter, to know for certain whether the ship was headed for a planet circling the yellow sun or one circling the neighbouring, orange sun of the system. Or even the tiny red sun of Proxima Centauri, further out. Somehow, starship dwellers had to make their goal clearer to these exotic beings, who operated in such mysterious ways. *But how?* Zakarov pondered.

'Thanks old guy. Are you able to make contact with these creatures at will?'

'Impossible for me to say. The timing has no regularity, so much depends on the phase.'

A Chihuahua ran out of the forest and headed toward the stretch of open ground that marked Yurchenko's front yard, as it made its way home in the pouring thunder storm. The cute little dog looked scruffy and bedraggled. It ran toward the house, leaping up onto the veranda.

'Ritchie! It's about time,' the old man said.

He stroked his four legged companion, sat on the floor besides him. The dog barked a couple of times, demanding more affection from his master. Yurchenko lifted the Chihuahua up with both his hands, and placed him onto his lap.

Zakarov continued, 'Well, the next time you meet these guys, try to reassure them we are not headed to Alpha Centauri A, god damn it. We are on our way to visit New Earth. The world that is most like the one we're from originally, circling their *neighbouring* sun. Can you do that?'

'I have no means for telling them anything. The communication is only one way,' Yurchenko replied flatly, and continued to affectionately stroke his pet.

Zakarov shrugged. 'Well, whatever.'

It was shortly after midnight and the present

generation's youngsters were partying with loud music and dance at the noisy Utopian Empire nightclub, on the west end of central Utopia. The music echoing and reverberating between walls of the large dance hall was the middle part of the tuneful disco track 'Resurrection' (by the twenty first century Russian band PPK). On a far side wall at the back of the dance hall there was a large screen, showing a view of our distant Sun as seen from one of the starship's observation decks. Swirling clouds of smoke and variable heating inside the hall, made the yellow speck of light appear to twinkle, more or less in rhythm to the disco tune.

'Jack, honey I've got a splitting headache. I'm gonna call it a night,' Alissa shouted into the ear drum of her boyfriend, struggling to get heard above the thumping rhythm.

'The night is still young, things have hardly begun. We'd be seen as party poopers,' he shouted back at her.

'I'm not gonna argue. Just tell me the drive code for the rover,' said the girl, sounding impatient.

He shrugged. 'Okay, you win. Let's go home.'

He took one last swig from the bottle in his hand.

Moments later, they were driving in a station wagon style rover, along the main high street in central Utopia. The road ahead of them glowed with a soft, moonlit-style of city centre lighting that created an eerie ambience across the derelict street. Jack was on, what could have been called, the driving seat of the partially autonomous vehicle. They were both feeling a little drowsy, having had one too many vodka spirit mixers at the Utopian Empire.

The rover did not keep to its side of the road and Alissa was getting impatient.

'Jack, are you sure you don't want *me* to drive?' She asked, sarcastically.

He glanced briefly at her, and then back toward the road in front again.

'Are you tryin' to tell me something here, Missy?' Said the blonde haired man. He shrugged and then chuckled recklessly, still under the influence of liquor.

'Just put the f****** thing on auto. You're too drunk.'

He took no heed, and carried on driving as he was.

At the next cross roads, Jack swung the rover right, into Lakeview Road. That made the driving a little uphill, as this half of Utopia's relief profile ascended from the Eridanus Valley, that ran through the centre of the city.

As they headed further out towards the suburbs, the roadside became densely forested on both sides and the intervals between street lamps grew longer, dimming light levels overall. The air inside the vehicle was filled with a faint, resinous odour coming from ancient evergreens that towered over in their varieties in the surrounding forests. The roadside was dark, and deadly silent.

For some unknown reason, gradually the scene ahead of them started to grow murky, as an engulfing cloud of mist began to condense out of the otherwise crystal clear, night air. Jack was falling asleep at the wheel, and the rover started drifting again. It appeared to be speeding up in fact, and Alissa's patience was wearing thin.

'My god Jack, slow down!' She screamed.

Too late. Before he could respond with any kind of braking on the vehicle, the pack of wolf angels had swooped in front, sending its autonomous steering mechanism wildly out of control. The rover veered off this way then that, and eventually hit the wooden post of a street lamp on the sidewalk. Alissa and Jack were knocked unconscious, having suffered major head injuries.

Later, in the critical care unit of the Med, they were both pronounced dead.

Zayna and Sharuk were fast asleep, with light from the top of the stairs hall way flooding into the bedroom. Zayna stirred in her sleep, as the nightmare began to take its course.

In her dream, she was sitting all by herself at her usual work station in the starship's silent control room. The main screen revealed a forward view of the ship, with the starfield depicted on it slowly rotating as the *Princess* turned in her artificial gravity spin. Alpha Centauri sparkled brilliantly at its centre, its intense yellow light creating a faint halo around the eight-spoked, telescopic image.

Then, gradually, the screen started to go murky and also wavy at the same time, reminiscent of how gentle ripples in a pond can cause reflections to become animated. Eventually, the murky expanse of cosmic darkness blotted out all the stars on the screen, and gradually condensed into the shape of the phantom beasts. They had arrived for her, she sensed. Gazing deeper into the screen, as if it were an unglazed portal into some alternate reality, Zayna was gripped by a peculiar urge to transcend its physical framework.

Slowly, she found herself drawn out of the chair where she sat and walking towards the large screen, as if the mysterious creatures looming large within it were somehow controlling her body and will.

As she got closer, suddenly the lead wolf angel sprung out of the screen with a menacing growl and grabbed her by the throat with its clawed hands. She could feel herself suffocating in the strangling hold, as it swung her body violently from side to side, lifting her off the floor. It snarled at her, exposing teeth and fangs. She looked into the archangel's piercing red, evil eyes. As the pain became agonising, with the creature's nails digging deeper into the sides of her throat like razors, she awoke from the nightmare, screaming loudly. Sharuk too was awake by now and he could see the blood gushing out of her throat, covering the white sheets and pillow in an intense blanket of red.

'Jesus Zayna! Oh my god…' He shouted, horrified and panic-stricken. 'Just stay there, don't move. I'll call for help.'

He leapt out of bed and struggled with the wristcom on the wooden dressing table, nearby.

UTOPIA CITY LIMITS
Please Switch Off Headlights

Next day, Zed Lincoln appeared on TV screens right across Utopia, with an emergency announcement.

'...even though we are headed to a planet in the neighbouring system to the one they're on, somehow, the creatures have mistakenly sensed us to be a future threat to their world. As a result, they are now attacking us from all directions with even greater ferocity. We have taken the emergency decision to maintain full daylight for twenty four hours around the clock, within the perimeter marked out by Utopia city limits...'

Irene and Razia were watching this as an interruption to the routine children's programming. They were in the back room of the ground floor, at Razia's house in Midsummer Crescent.

'Wow, cool. Just imagine, we no longer have to go to bed at night,' Razia said.

'You're kidding me, right?' Irene replied, quizzically.

'Kind of. Although you couldn't really go to sleep in daylight, I mean not properly.'

'Trust me, you will if you were sleepy enough.'

'What about the spooky wolf angels?' Razia asked.

'Ooh, don't mention them, puhleeze!' Irene exclaimed, shuddering at the very thought.

Razia glanced outside into the long garden that stretched all the way down to the lake, at the back of their house. The willow trees were swaying and the rain drops that had collected on the long blades of grass on the lawn, sparkled in the morning sunshine.

'It's stopped raining and the winds have picked up again. Let's go and fly our kites,' she suggested cheerfully.

'Okay. I'll have to borrow your golden striped one again though, 'cos mines is at home,' Irene said.

'No problemo.'

The two girls launched their diamond-shaped, remote controlled kites from the stretch of lawn in Razia's back garden. Nano-sized radio receivers, actuators, motors,...and other bits of technology were finely embedded into the fabric of the kites, that subtlely responded to propulsive commands sent from the ground via wristcoms. The girls watched them fly higher and higher, going up all the way into the dark sky. Irene's blue kite, striped in gold, flew the highest. It rose past the top of the local miniature sun, as it glided on the back of a strong, gusty breeze. Once above the 'sunlit level', i.e. past the height of miniature suns, the kites were no longer illuminated by under-lighting; the miniature suns only beamed their rays downwards onto the landscape. To aid visibility in the dark skies above, the kites were equipped with tiny light emitting diodes, which lit up their diamond shaped outlines in a luminous red.

'Oh, look. There's a beautiful rainbow,' said Razia, as she peered in the direction of the azure coloured lake, over in the distance.

Through some unique combinations of the angle of light coming from the miniature suns towering high above on their transparent pedestals, and the misty spray of localised rain drizzling over the lake, the rainbow was seen to arch *upwards* into the sky.

'That's an awesome sight. I'll guide my kite in that direction,' Irene agreed.

'I'm gonna take a picture,' Razia said, levelling her wristcom toward the sky to take the shot. 'Cool snap. One for me to show my mommy.'

The two girls watched the skies in wonder.

Inside the house, Rujina and Shirin, who was Razia's mum, continued to watch the sombre TV announcement. Following Zed Lincoln's message, the program had moved on to report on the latest casualties and underlined the severity of the nightmare syndrome. Reactions from people in every section of the community showed the whole thing to be hanging like a dark and sinister cloud above the *Centauri Princess'* interior.

'I'm just totally gutted by all of this. I mean, why the heck didn't those great great great grand parents of ours do some homework, before deciding that it would be safe to send their descendants on such a lengthy journey, huh?' Rujina said, looking uneasy. She walked up and down the length of the room, trying to ease the nerves.

'Me too.' Shirin replied. 'I'm sure they did do some homework, and anticipated all kinds of weird and wonderful possibilities. But even in their wildest imaginations, I bet they could never have guessed about *this*,' she speculated. 'I mean, even if we had *photon torpedoes* or *light sabres* of the kind they used in old fashioned sci-fi fantasy movies, I doubt if we could use them on the wolf angels.'

'I guess you've got a point. It's pretty hard to know every single thing you'll have to contend with on a long and daring voyage like this, out into the complete unknown. Makes me shudder just thinkin' about it. I'm gonna ask the girls to come back in now.' Rujina said.

She headed for the kitchen, at the back of the house, that led out into the garden. On her way, she passed Cutie, Razia's pet budgerigar, which was perched on the inside edge of its cage. The cute little bird slanted its head to one side and eyed Rujina, uttering a few shrilling sounds as if trying to make conversation. She ignored it altogether, and headed out.

In the garden, the gusty breeze had increased its strength to a howling gale, signalling the arrival of another storm. The azure waters of the lake, seen over in the distance, had become choppy. Light from miniature suns nearby had been dimmed, temperatures feeling lower, as the ambience was auto adjusted by CPC to mimic natural conditions normally experienced ahead of the arrival of a storm of this kind.

'Girls! I'd like you both back inside the house now please. There's more bad weather coming our way,' Rujina shouted across the extensive lawn.

'Razia's kite is stuck on the tree, mom. We can't bring it back down,' Irene shouted back.

The orange kite was stranded in midst of the branches of a willow tree, its ribboned tail rigidly wrapped around a few dead twigs, near the top of the crown. It made a rustling sound in the gusts that swept through the thick, drooping foliage.

'Okay, hang about. I'll get Number 232,' Rujina said and went back inside the house. She told Shirin of the predicament with the kite.

The advanced, people-friendly repairbot specially allocated to serve Shirin's home, was busy spraying house plants that were growing inside large hanging baskets in the kitchen. They were suspended from the tall ceiling, and were mostly filled with a special variety of colourful-flowering orchids; Shirin having a particular love for the exotic species.

'Number 232, I'd like you to quit this task for now, please. Can you go out into the garden and fetch Razia's kite that's stuck on the tree top?' Shirin asked.

Number 232 turned its head around. Its mechanical eye lids blinked a couple of times.

'Sure. No sweat,' it said in a friendly, virtually human, tone and glided out of the house.

The little pet robot was highly articulated in its design. It had its own built in, self-refuelling compressed air thrusters and helicopter-like rotor blades for propeller, that enabled it to glide effortlessly and with precision, through the air.

It flew up to the top of the tall willow tree and retrieved the kite, releasing it back into the air, from where Razia regained control using her wristcom as a remote control unit.

Both Shirin and Rujina had a common ancestry linking them to the Bangladesh region of the Indian sub-continent back on Earth, and their well defined features hinted at this. They also had just one child each, which was below the norm; two children per couple was the most commonly adopted family profile across the ship's wider population. This number kept the equilibrium just right. For every one death, there would be one new birth. Effective control of population growth was an essential prerequisite on this multi-generational voyage, traversing the enormous light years of space and taking the vast aeons of time to do so.

The starship's 'miniature Earth' ecosystem model, with a biosphere volume of just over eleven hundred cubic kilometres, permitted a maximum population size of up to five thousand people. Beyond that number, there would be a whole raft of problems. For example, the starship interior could not supply sufficient food from the farming complex to meet the nutritional needs, and the delicate balance of oxygen/CO_2 between plant and animal life across the interior, would be disrupted. Beyond those, the recycling drivers for household waste and water were also designed to operate within a model that worked to predefined, maximum people-numbers.

Thanks to the tightly managed procedures in place, the starship's total population had never wandered beyond a minimum of eight hundred and a maximum of three thousand persons over the past two thousand years since the start of the mission. Birth control was medically introduced into the female of the species from an early age. A minor operation was compulsory for all girls between the ages of five and ten. This simply suspended their reproductive capacity to a default 'off' status after they reached puberty. Later on in life, when they got married or decided to settle down into a permanent family oriented relationship, the status could be momentarily reversed through a second, minor operation.

The other issue was of course maintaining a wide enough gene pool, with such a small population. Whereas here on Earth we have several races of humans spanning a globe of several billion, where successive generations are able to spread the gene pool widely, such luxuries never existed in the enclosed mini-world onboard the ship. It was a well known fact in biology and medical science, that if an enclosed society did not have a large enough gene pool across a wide population, then diseases and harmful viruses simply did not get a chance to become 'diluted out' through successive generations. The problem of 'inbreeding' thus causing birth defects, allergies and all manner of other problems for the later generations.

Mission designers for the *Centauri Princess*, prior to her launch from Earth, had originally worked out a solution to this that consisted of two separate measures. Firstly, the initial passenger make up was taken from a planet wide population. This meant selecting people from every single race scattered across all the continents of Earth, ranging from Africans, through Hispanics to Chinese, as passengers for the mission.

The second, and more contentious part of the solution, required the ship to take a reserve bank of frozen eggs and sperm from a much wider gene pool, on initial departure from Earth. The *Centauri Princess'* central nervous system, CPC, then monitored births and deaths along the voyage for each person/family/generation. Based on records being maintained on an ongoing basis, it calculated after roughly how many natural births along a particular genetic line one needed to expand one's gene pool. The ship's medical team then advised passengers when they ought to start drawing on the frozen fertility ingredients.

It should be noted that only *one* member of a couple needed to resort to the frozen fertility ingredient during any one particular pregnancy; that way, half of the offspring would be genetically natural in the relationship. This made the scheme more universally acceptable across all communities with their highly varied, individual moral and religious beliefs.

The success of that regime was presently reflected in how healthy and normal both Irene and Razia were in their day to day livelihoods, with absolutely no loss of immunity to any of the hereditary diseases passed on from earlier generations. Without its successful administration, given the tiny size of population, the present generation would have inbred hundreds of times over that expected for natural gene pools here on Earth. As a result, starship dwellers would have been all diseased—and probably too weak—to continue the immensely long voyage.

On account of his deep fascination with astronomy, Zakarov had suggested Joey be the one to go and visit

Azura at the DSTF this time round, to gain insights on a new discovery in the Alpha Centauri system. He jumped at the opportunity, thinking it would be good for his own personal development.

Joey was at home preparing for the trip. He stuffed a pair of magnetic-soled shoes into his backpack along with various other odds and ends, that included a writing pad for taking notes and a silver pen that had been specially designed for writing under conditions of total weightlessness. And - not forgetting - two bottles of pina colada, as he was sure to feel dry along the way.

'I still can't believe Alissa and Jack are gone. This thing's gone way out of hand now,' Alcyone said, staring out of the first floor window.

'You're totally convinced that their death is linked to the nightmares, aren't you? But didn't the post mortem report merely state 'severe head injuries, during a fatal rover accident'?' Joey said.

'I don't know what to believe anymore, Joey. All I know is what my instincts are telling me. The MMC probably aren't telling us the full truth. Not in every situation.'

'You look so uptight about it, sweet heart. You just need to lighten up a bit and relax.'

He walked over to her and held her from behind, wrapping his arms around in a comforting embrace.

'So what's this 'great' discovery at Alpha Centauri all about then?' Alcyone said, turning around to face him.

'Ah, ha! That's what I'm gonna find out.'

'You sound pretty excited.'

'I am. Not too excited about meeting that Azura guy, though. Been hearing things about him.'

Alcyone chuckled.

'Honestly Joey...I'm sure he doesn't bite!'

'No he doesn't. He does worse. He looks down on people—and lowers them with his superior intellectual reasonings.'

'He can't do that to you. You seem to know all your astronomy.'

'Maybe. But the guy's a well respected genius in his field.'

'Well in that case—I wish you all the luck, mister,' Alcyone said, with a warm smile.

Joey boarded the extended elevator system that ran from an underground terminal at the centre of Utopia, going all the way to that far outpost of the DSTF, located some nine miles away near the starship's front. The journey was to take a long, twenty five minutes, and it would have been extremely rare for him to have found any company on this deserted route. Fortunately, to help cut the boredom, the elevator was wired to CPC throughout the journey and offered a range of music, TV and interactive video entertainment. Joey tuned into his favourite game of virtual tennis and continued the tournament that he had started with CPC back in the control room, in his day job.

At the back of his mind though, he also felt quite nervous. Azura was a well known boffin, who was also projected to have somewhat of an inflated ego. Whilst the visit would be good for gaining experience, Joey also feared that Azura could put him on the spot with difficult questions. He had done as much preparatory homework as possible, having consulted widely. He knew the basic score with the wolf angels syndrome and all the popular theories about their origination from the Alpha Centauri system, from people like Crista, Yurchenko, Chang and of course Zakarov himself. Still…he felt nervous.

The extended elevator system, that ran beyond the biosphere limits of the ship, operated on a mechanism that varied between wires and wheels; for the wires part, it resembled a mountain climbing ski lift here on Earth, whereas for the wheels part, it was more like an isolated compartment of the starship's mono rail shuttle train. At this moment, the elevator was passing through the Restricted Zone of the *Centauri Princess*, and Joey looked out to see if he could spot anything unusual in that secretive zone.

The Restricted Zone took up a huge volume of the ship's total space, enclosed between the biosphere's Great Front Wall and the starship's nose cone, past the DSTF. In order to keep to an 'open and honest' policy, the MMC's formally declared purpose of the Restricted Zone was simply to securely hold a large stockpile of radioactive nuclear warheads, that could be used for defence against any potential alien encounters. But given how closely guarded it was and the clandestine nature of its contents, over the generations, a few folks had formed certain beliefs concerning its possible other hidden purposes. The most popular of these was that, in addition to holding some warheads, it also contained cryogenic compartments where the bodies of the starship's first president, Joseph Lexington, and his clan were kept in some form of suspended animation. Rumours had it that, contrary to public knowledge, they may have found a secret solution to keeping people in a permanent state of hibernation after all, and key members of the original crew would be reawakened when the mission eventually reached New Earth, some time in the far distant future. *Those were just uninformed speculations, of course.* Whatever additional secrets were hidden inside the Restricted Zone, they were certainly beyond the knowledge of anyone within Joey's sphere of contact. The entities in the present generation who were deemed to know the full truth were: the computer system, CPC, Zed Lincoln and perhaps one or two of his closest and most senior MMC officials.

As the elevator passed through the central portion of the Zone, for about a minute or two, Joey could have sworn he'd felt a marginal drop in temperatures inside the compartment where he was sitting. It was only a tiny drop - but still noticeable. He wondered if that could be down to a draft of cold air coming from the suspected cryogenic compartments? Through the elevator's glazed window he saw nothing more than the grey, metallic wall that sealed in the controversial zone's contents. Joey decided the experience was far too subtle and transient for him to make any kind of a firm deduction.

Eventually, his elevator reached the distant control room of the DSTF and Dermot Azura was there to greet him.

'Hello Joey. I was hoping Zakarov would come over, but it's good to have you here, anyhow,' he said, as the two men shook hands.

Joey felt annoyed. A nice start that. Azura certainly

knew how to make people feel welcome. *Zakarov would have been a more important person to see this ground-breaking discovery, but you will do. What a snob!* Joey thought.

Zayna had lost a fair amount of blood between her gruesome nightmare ordeal and arrival at the Med. Her condition was later stabilised through a series of transfusions, administered from the limited blood bank. Having an ancestry linking back to the Arabian peninsular on Earth, she possessed a very rare blood type, making it next to impossible to find a suitable blood donor within the starship's limited population. She knew how fortunate she was for the Med to have kept her unique blood group as part of the limited supply.

There was a knock on the door of the ward where she was presently recovering.

'Come in,' she said in a broken voice, sounding faint.

Zakarov and Lucy both entered the room, smiling warmly.

'Hello Zayna, good to hear that you have been making steady progress,' Lucy said, walking up to her and giving her a gentle hug.

Zayna was sitting up on the bed, wearing a purple robe that served as the hospital gown. Her neck and throat were covered in a multiple layered, thickly wound bandage, that concealed the injuries.

'Yeah, one of our angels is missing from the control room,' Zakarov added, light heartedly.

'Making progress, maybe. Still get such real flashes of that confrontation now and again. It's just too much to bear,' Zayna said, looking sulky.

Lucy had brought a bunch of freshly cut, scented flowers, a box of chocolates and a get well card. Zakarov was holding out the large presentation box that contained them all.

'Here, we brought you these,' Lucy said, placing the presents on the bedside table and handing her the get well card.

Zayna opened the card and her face brightened slightly as she browsed all the thoughtful messages inside, from just about everyone she knew.

'I'm really chuffed,' she said.

There was a brief silence, as she continued scanning the card.

'I don't see my boyfriend here...and he never comes to visit me—'

She broke into tears. Lucy rushed to her side.

'I'm sorry Zayna, I guess it's rather insensitive of him. But hey, we're here for you and if you ever want anything, just shout.'

Zayna sobbed quietly, still weak from her injuries.

Caroline entered the room with some fresh bandages in a tray.

'I'm sorry folks, but this is where I have to ask you to leave,' she said in a doctor's voice.

'Fresh bandages? We were about to, Dr. Polansky,' Zakarov said light heartedly, as he and Lucy exited the room.

Caroline did not know whether to feel sympathetic, angry or envious toward the woman who'd effectively stolen the love of her life - *she thought she had.*

'Look, I wasn't to know. He never said anything about you...' Zayna said, nervously.

'You don't have to apologise to me Zayna. Really, if you guys can make something of it, I'm happy for you,' Caroline snapped, knowing full well that having a convicted criminal for a lover was never going to be a smart or a lasting move for anybody.

Sympathetic? Yes. She decided that's what she felt most for this seemingly innocent victim of a cruel and deceitful, two-timing bastard.

The sports and leisure complex was an area specially set aside in the open prairies of the Upper Province, where various games and recreational sports were accommodated. Its main building housed a large gymnasium and a number of indoor swimming pools, along with various other, less formal games like snooker, pools and ten pin bowling.

For outdoor activities, there was a 'crazy golfing' course, an athletics ring, a paraglider launch site and a large lake for rowing and other water sports that became especially popular during the summer season. Of all of these activities, paragliding—not surprisingly—was always the most popular, as it offered many thrills inside a cylindrically shaped, rotating world of the *Centauri Princess'* type.

A paraglider could launch himself into a controlled flight path that would take him to enormous heights above the interior, given the zero gravity that would be experienced once airborne. Climbing ever higher on the back of naturally rising thermals, one would eventually reach a point of some three miles in altitude, from where a breathtaking, 3D panoramic view of the curved interior could be seen. A look along the length of the starship from such an optimum vantage point would reveal its entire cylindrical shape, with aerial views running from floor to ceiling of all the forests and settlements, seen curving along the sides. And of course, depending on the direction one was facing, straight ahead in the distance there would always be a circular outline of either the Great Front Wall or the Great Rear Wall of the ship, shining dimly with a dull, metallic grey colour.

Chang and Crista were playing a round of crazy golf outdoors in the sports and leisure complex, a couple of miles beyond Utopia city limits. Since the changing gravity vectors on the ship made life difficult for the sport to be played properly in the conventional way, it had always been prefixed by the word 'crazy' for as long as anyone could remember.

Crista oriented himself so that he faced the direction in which the floor of the ship was moving in its gravity rotation, and positioned the ball on the marked spot on the grass ready for his first go. He swung the club hard and hit it, so that the ball went upwards on a sixty degree inclined trajectory, relative to the local horizon. The two men watched as it arched up, towards the sky. At the top of its flight, it basically hovered there, in mid air for a while. Eventually, passing high above their heads, it gently glided down onto a stretch of grass about a hundred yards away, close to the flag pole that marked the hole.

That spot was way behind where Chang and Crista stood, talking.

'You know, I've been thinking lately how they never got to build sleeper ships in the end,' said Crista, looking rather distant and deep in intellectual thought.

'Oh? What do you mean?' Chang asked, puzzled.

'You know, the alternatives to an ark ship, where you could put people into suspended animation…wake them up on arrival at their destination…that kind of thing.'

'You don't think Lexington and his clan sleeping inside Restricted Zone…I mean, no truth to the speculation?' Chang asked, with an obvious hint of humour in his tone.

'I'll take that witticism lightly. Who knows? No, I'm talking about the *real* science of suspended animation, in the context of interstellar journeys.'

'It could haf been done, if they continue research that they started,' Chang said. 'I mean with nano-technologies, anything possible. But then—it been darn complicated.'

'I guess people had eventually woken up to the complexities involved and how you could never stop the ageing process just like that. When the human genome project was first completed a couple of thousand years ago, with later advances in cloning and such like, they thought they'd cracked the mysteries of life once and for all. That humans could be re-engineered to do anything. How wrong they were,' said Crista.

'Yes but cloning help out with longer life span, using fresh organ every time. People live longer.'

'Cloning of human organs did appear to help, and for a couple of centuries, people benefited. Later on though, when the super viruses appeared on the scene and the technological and environmental collapse started, things really started to get out of hand. Permanently altering the course of nature by such means as genetic manipulation of viruses and 'playing god' with cellular re-engineering of simple life forms, all had unknown consequences that back-fired big time in the end. Viruses will mutate and evolve according to their own naturally guided evolutionary paths beyond the wishes and desires of mankind. Nature always seemed to have had an inbuilt programming to keep these things a few steps ahead of the game, no matter what counter measures were devised against them. Besides, even at the height of all medical advances, they were still a million miles away from any form of *true* suspended animation or 'sleep immortality', as I like to call it,' Crista explained, coming back to suspended animation after digressing from the topic.

'From technical point of view, it stand with reason. If suspended animation to work, you haf to stop every single cell in human body from multiplying. If human cloning to work, you haf to keep integrity of underlying programming in copying everything. And how complex is human or animal cell compare to simple bacteria or even perhaps a virus?' Chang agreed. 'Of course, that not to say if we find a future technology miracle, suspended animation could just work. But that wishing thought only for now.'

'Plain, wishful thinking on the part of some people. There are as many atoms making up one molecule of DNA as there are as many stars in an entire galaxy. *The number of bits of instructions it takes to define a complete human being is nearly a million times more than the number of bits it takes to define a simple virus.* At the time of Earth departure, we were still a long way from completely modelling the anatomical evolution of more deadly viruses like HIV. And we're still some way off from that. Yet a virus is so simple that it is not even classed as a true life form, as such. So, to go from bioengineering a virus…to suspending the ageing process of a human…was never a realistic proposition to begin with. Many think-tanks had devised 'magic potions' along the way, but when they administered their patients - no that should be called *victims* - with the drugs, they gave their subjects *cancer* instead of longevity! Of course that did not stop the debates from raging rather violently when they started constructing this ship. In the end, they woke up to the realities and had to settle for the multi-generational mission concept, with a biosphere and artificially maintained natural ecosystem - like what we have here,' Crista said, as the two men walked across the golf course.

Crista aimed to deliver a 'hole in one' with his next shot, now that the ball was only around ten yards or so from the flag pole. He carefully aligned the club, judging things by eye, and gently hit the ball. It rolled along nicely at first, but missed the hole by a couple of inches.

'Yes, but think about mess we're in now. If we were suspended, we could sleep through all this nightmare bullshit nonsense! No?' Chang said and grinned.

'Ah, but then we would have missed out on all the adventures, like this wonderful game of crazy golfing that we're enjoying here. Think how utterly *boring* it would have been to leave one Earth back there, sleep through the whole journey, simply to wake up and step out of your ship onto another Earth, virtually the same as the one you'd left behind, in a neighbouring solar system. Boring!'

They laughed lightly at the thought, and continued the afternoon round of crazy golfing.

The other option was of course fast, fractions of light-speed missions. Originally, many had argued that by inventing faster and faster means of propulsion, one could cross the interstellar gulf separating Sol from its nearest neighbouring system within a single human life span. Proponents of that line of thinking worked on countless theoretical concepts that offered the promise of high speed missions. The popular ones amongst them were the solar sail, matter/anti-matter, magnetic plasma propulsion and Project Orion.

In the end, the high-speed mode of interstellar travel turned out to be a 'catch-22' situation; if you travelled at ten per cent light-speed (the maximum most theoretical concepts ever projected in the era when the *Centauri Princess* was being built) then your speed would be a staggering, thirty thousand kilometres per second. Moving at that speed you would require massive amounts of shielding against potential micro-meteoroids; you would be covering a distance three times the diameter of the Earth in one second...even a grain of cosmic dust will pose a major hazard. When one is travelling that fast, anticipating and dodging any objects in the ship's path of travel would be inconceivable, and space between the stars is far from empty.

The individual Oort clouds that surround our Sun and Alpha Centauri overlap in the middle, and there is simply too much uncharted material floating around in the interstellar dark to set a safe course that avoided all the myriad of cometary bodies and gas and dust remnants left over from the original formation of each system.

If you hit a comet at anything higher than snail's pace, you're vapourised into oblivion. If you increase the shielding for micrometeroids, then you increase spacecraft mass, which would make it impossible for you to accelerate to those kinds of speeds in the first place. Even if you travelled at just one per cent light-speed (which would still make it virtually impossible to dodge any interstellar debris), then you still need four hundred and thirty years or seventeen consecutive generations to make the one way trip to Alpha Centauri. To accommodate the day to day livelihood for seventeen consecutive generations, you need a substantial biosphere on your starship. If you have a biosphere, then you're talking of a very large scale vessel and you will need refuelling, at least for water, if not for anything else.

Eventually, all of the above considerations, plus the technically insurmountable issues with suspended animation, made the multi-generational, interstellar ark mode of 'slow' transport the most viable way for humanity to cross the light years. And the art of successfully mining bodies within overlapping Oort clouds for meeting life support, starship propulsion and raw materials needs, made crossing the 'virtual bridge' to New Earth in the Alpha Centauri system the first choice extra-solar system destination for humanity.

And what were the early thoughts for the existence of an Earth-like world on the nearest cosmic shores beyond our solar system? And for such an overlapping Oort cloud scenario to exist between it and us, that could neither be seen telescopically from Earth nor verified by mathematical calculations with any degree of certainty? Well, for those scientists who were prepared to lean just a tiny tiny bit towards religion — and were willing to take an optimistic view — it boiled down to this simple fact: if god had given mankind stars in the night sky to serve as anything more than celestial 'light shows' merely for its amusement, then he will have provided such a world, along with a nice trail of comets and planetoids that could act as 'stepping stones' for fuel and power, starting at the Kuiper belt in our solar system, and going all the way into the heart of the Alpha Centauri system. He will have provided such an enigmatic avenue of escape, on the extreme fringes of human reasoning and acceptability, for no more compelling a reason than the simple truth: *that god always works in mysterious ways...*

Religion aside though, ever since the 1950s astronomers have hypothesised - and steadfastly held onto - the idea of Oort clouds existing around our Sun and other stars. Recent studies of nearby stars from space-based telescopes like the Hubble have shown disks of cometary and asteroidal material swirling around them in far greater abundance and stretching farther out into space than hitherto thought possible. In specific directions, these clouds act like 'virtual bridges' extending out into space, silently beckoning to the inhabitants of worlds in neighbouring planetary systems to cross the interstellar gulf with far more ease than they might have otherwise imagined possible.

Furthermore, with the advent of computers and faster processing power, dynamical models simulated in the late twentieth century had amply demonstrated that both of Alpha Centauri's principal suns were capable of holding Earth-like rocky planets within their habitable zones, without them suffering any adverse impacts from the gravitational complexity of the binary set-up.

Azura was showing Joey a multi-spectral image plate, that had captured the new planet-like body circling around Alpha Centauri A. Using the DSTF's most sophisticated and penetrating features, it had been determined to be a giant Earth-sized "moon", which revolved around the Jovian planet. The duo, in turn, circled the yellow (primary) sun of the system in an orbit that was centrally placed within the habitable zone.

'So that's the home planet where they live?' Joey asked, referring to the tiny speck of light on the image. He decided he had very little choice but to tolerate Azura's boffin-style cynicisms, and make the most out of his visit.

'That's the theory. So far, we have evidence from all of our scientific research conducted here at the DSTF, and also the psychoanalysis reports from…your friend, you know, the guy who lives in the Black Forest?' Azura laughed lightly.

'Yurchenko?' Joey replied. He could sort of see the humour behind Azura's laugh, having known the pseudo scientific methods that Yurchenko practised.

'Yeah, that's him. Although I believe it was Crista and Dr. Chang at the Med who first came up with the hypo, so they deserve the credit.'

Azura was wrong there. It was Yurchenko who deserved the credit. He was the scientific visionary who had been asserting his hypothesis about the wolf angels' planet for years, but Joey was not going to argue with Azura. It wouldn't really be worth the effort.

'Dr. Azura, tell me something. In your own opinion, why is there an eighty year oscillation in the intensity of nightmares reported going back across past generations? Could there be a genuine connection between our nightmares and the binary orbital period between Alpha Centauri A and B?' Joey asked, remembering that Zakarov and Crista had briefed him on that the other day, over lunch.

'You ask an interesting question, young Joey.' Azura replied, like a father talking to his son.

Joey felt slightly belittled by the tone, but kept quiet.

'There could well be. The truth of the matter is we don't really know for certain. We know that the system is a lot older than our ancestors' parent star of Sol and that the life forms evolving there are ahead of us by a billion years or so in terms of evolutionary development.'

'Are you able to make a wild speculation?' Joey insisted.

Azura thought for a moment and then wandered across the control room to a small console in the far corner.

'Here, have a look at this.'

Joey followed him across, carefully treading under the minimal gravity conditions of the DSTF, and anchored himself onto the swivel chair next to Azura. The DSTF's chief pulled up a graphic on the greenish display screen, having selected a few options from CPC's DSTF-interface.

'This model is one that a member of my team put together a few years ago. It shows that there is a tiny tiny

—but appreciable—amplitude variation in the total bolometric radiation output from star A, which oscillates with an eighty year period.'

'That's interesting, but what are we to conclude from such an observation?' Joey asked, looking rather puzzled.

'What do *you* reckon? Think hard.'

Azura put him on the spot, something he had feared might happen all along. Joey thought for a moment, carefully searching his vocabulary for the right words before replying.

'There is somehow a link between the energy output of their sun and the severity with which they could threaten people in their nightmares?'

Azura smiled. 'You are a smart one, Joey, that's exactly the hypo that I put forward to fit the observations.'

He stood up and wandered across the room again, as he found it easier to explain things whilst on his feet.

'The wolf angels somehow draw energy from the unique and complex arrangement between the yellow and orange suns in their binary system. I have two theories which describe the possibilities here. The first theory is that *the two suns induce minute amounts of flaring activity in their mutual gravitational interactions*, as they revolve about their common centre of gravity every eighty years. The wolf angels somehow thrive on the back of those, becoming stronger when the suns are at their closest; weaker when they are at their furthest apart,' he said, and paused.

'The second theory is that *they draw upon the changing*

levels of illumination coming from their night sky. We know the two suns range in distance between eleven and thirty six AUs from each other, as they revolve in a highly elliptical orbit, every eighty years. This means the K-type, orange sun of Alpha Centauri B shines in the night skies of the wolf angels' home planet with an intensity that is *eleven times greater* when the two suns are closest together, compared to when they are furthest apart. My theory is that this oscillating range somehow affects their energy levels.'

'Dr. Azura, those are the most fascinating things I've ever heard in my long interests in astronomy,' Joey said, with genuine amazement.

Azura sighed. 'But they're only theoretical speculations, you must remember.'

'They sound perfectly plausible, though. I wonder if there are any other examples, to our knowledge, of this kind of deep interconnection between life forms thriving on a world and the subtle variations of light from celestial bodies nearby, in their system?' Joey said.

'Well...let's see now,' Azura thought for a moment, tapping into his wealth of astronomical knowledge. 'Ah, of course. The Moon. Back on our ancestor's home planet of Earth - perfect example. The queen of the night shines with a regular variation of light, as she goes through her phases every twenty nine days. Believe it or not, that silvery wonder of the night skies of Earth has had an enormous impact on the evolution of life on that far away world. Variations in the amount of moonlight bathing the surfaces of its vast oceans, has influenced the mating patterns of sea shells and other creatures of the dark. And it is even thought to have had an influence on the periodicity of the monthly menstrual cycle of Earth women.'

'Fascinating stuff. Perhaps I should not loathe the subject of 'Earth Studies' so much, after all!' Joey chuckled.

'You young people should generally take a bigger interest in the subject, it offers much to be learned,' Azura said. 'Isn't your father an avid follower of Earth-related topics? How is he these days?'

'He's fine.'

'Astronomy is not an *isolated* science you know. It touches on just about everything in some way or other,' Azura said.

'Philosophy and religion are included in this, right?'

'Definitely so. And even though I am not a religious man myself, I firmly accept that there is an underlying 'cosmic design' and an inherent 'cosmic connection' between widely separated elements in the fundamentals of creation, which we as scientists are prepared to overlook all too often.'

Azura was now digging way too deep in his intellectual lecturing and Joey struggled to keep up.

'The cosmic forces which mysteriously bind atoms and molecules of non-living matter into the double helix structure of the DNA's coded instructions, purely through the random passage of time is equally as perplexing as many other unexplained phenomena - gravity being an obvious example. The molecules that are vibrating with energy within the very cells of our own bodies, the photons of light emitted from every incandescent source in the universe...and the invisible threads of gravity holding the whole thing together…all share an intricate interconnection…'

He looked at Joey, who echoed back a somewhat blank and confused look. 'Sorry, I did not mean to go on.'

'No, I think it's all really fascinating stuff,' Joey said, hoping he did not sound too pretentious.

He was about to leave the control room of the DSTF, when he pondered one more question. Since he was unlikely to come this way again for a long time and Azura being the leading authority on the ship on such matters, he felt it to be pertinent to clear all lingering mysteries. His confidence with Azura had grown stronger; nervousness, easing.

'These wolf-like creatures live physically on their own planet, but they also have an energy component to their total existence, which gives them the capacity to roam freely across the night of interstellar space, right?' He asked, hoping he phrased that right.

'Yes, I think I get the gist of what you are trying to say so far, but do continue,' Azura encouraged.

'So what's there to say, they can't materialise on New Earth around their neighbouring star, and for them to have a presence on that planet too?'

'And we could be heading straight into the lion's den?' Azura laughed. 'Nonsense! If they could physically transport themselves across from their world to New Earth, then they would have physically invaded this ship too, and remained here permanently until they finished us off,' Azura explained, in as logical a way as he could master.

'But they cannot do that, you see. The wolf angels have evolved a psychic ability to merely project their images into space. And these images exist in an alternate dimension altogether, separate from our own physical dimension here. Hence, during the deepest part of our sleep, our brain's neural networks are somehow subtlely able to 'tune in' to those images, giving rise to nightmares. The only time when they can inflict any harm upon us or make their presence physically felt, is during those brief, transitory moments when their universe and our universe temporarily intersect each other, and share a common material plane of existence.'

'So New Earth is not infested by these creatures?'

'No. If it were, such a phenomenon would defy all rational logic known to us with our current science. And our observational evidence of comparing the life signatures between Earth, their world and New Earth confirms that.'

'By analysing the minute amounts of reflected light from their planet, we note that the life signatures we observe on their planet are radically different to those we observe on the Earth and New Earth, right?' Joey clarified.

'Absolutely. New Earth and our ancestors' Earth show identical—and benign—signatures of life in our telescopic studies.'

'So why did they not induce nightmares when the ship was still in the vicinity of Sol?'

'In their psychic state of existence as creatures of pure energy, the wolf angels fear high levels of light and other electromagnetic radiation. They struggle to form their presence when there are 'noisy' resonances from alternative sources, that distract them in that process.

That was how we were able to dampen the severity of nightmares by leaving lights on at night, around our homes.'

'I see. So they could never attack people in their dreams back on Earth. And, by the same token, they cannot attack anyone on New Earth in their energy state, because it circles very close to its parent star where there are high dosages of radiation. Well, that makes sense.' Joey had an obvious tone of fascination in his voice by now.

'Whilst the physical part of their total existence - the 'body and flesh' part - draws energy from interactions between their two suns and roams physically on their world, the 'pure energy' part that's projected way out into space, can only function in the dark. That is the part that we see in our nightmares as 'wolf angel' apparitions. And they can only roam in the depths of dark, interstellar space, away from the bright neighbourhood of any particular star.' Azura concluded.

Outside of Utopia's city limits, nightfall returned across the miniature world's interior in the normal way. Zed Lincoln and the MMC had obviously calculated that an 'end of nights' policy could only be worked in a sustainable way within Utopia itself. By limiting it to the built up areas of the ship, there would be no danger of disrupting the natural day/night cycle for the plants and wildlife thriving in the broader interior. It stood to reason that ninety five per cent of the starship population, who permanently lived in Utopia, would be afforded the highest level of immunity from nightmare-induced attacks by the mysterious creatures roaming in the interstellar night.

Historic records had it that, in a previous generation, the MMC once experimented with an unnatural day/night balance across the ecosystem, which resulted in a major disruption to the natural flowering and fruiting cycles of plants and had a hugely disruptive impact on animal behaviour. The generation presently enjoying the adventures of this epic journey, had absolutely no desire to go down that path again, whatever the cost.

Inside the vast perimeter fencing that circled the starship's farming complex, there thrived a small village community. It was made up of twenty two wooden-built houses running along a suburban street, with the settlement broadly resembling an average suburban street on the outskirts of Utopia. This was where the farming complex's permanent employee population lived, giving them convenient access to their places of work. Towards the rear and running parallel with the adjacent rows of houses, there were a couple of rows of barns, which contained a series of stables that housed the starship's two hundred-strong horse population.

Around midnight, by and large the farming complex's entire village community had fallen fast asleep, with lights left on inside their homes, as advised by the chief medical officer.

In the silence of the warm night, Karyn Colaco felt restless, as she lay awake next to her husband who seemed to be sleeping peacefully enough. On this night, she just could not fall asleep. No particular reason, for life had generally been good to the Colacos. They had the perfect marriage and she had a sound career as an instructor for would-be horse riders. Business was flourishing at her riding school, with people flocking in from Utopia and elsewhere across the interior.

Karyn turned on the bedside lamp and got up. She glanced across at a mirror that was mounted on the door of a wardrobe, next to the dressing table. It dimly reflected back her Mediterranean tanned face and azure coloured eyes. For a fifty one year old, she felt proud of her looks, having managed to keep the wrinkles from appearing up till now.

She had a dry feeling in her throat and wandered across to the first floor kitchen. She poured a glass of water from the dispenser. *I could read a novel. That should help me to fall asleep*, she thought, gulping chilled water.

She curled up in bed with a paperback called 'The Planet of a Million Suns'. The volume looked dated, its pages yellow. Written in some distant, forgotten era of the *Centauri Princess'* epic voyage, it conveyed the intriguing thoughts and messages of its writer. They were perfectly preserved in this simple media of written words imprinted onto paper. A long perished author spoke silently to Karyn, through the corridors of time, as she became absorbed into the opening paragraphs of his writings. Those were the things that captured Karyn's imagination most in all her readings, as she was primarily a collector of old books.

As she was half way down the first page, she felt a slight breeze brush along her left cheek, coming through the half open bedroom window. She took a glance toward the curtains, dimly lit by the bedside lamp. They appeared to flutter very gradually with the incoming breeze. Suddenly there was a faint hissing sound, out on the street. Karyn strained her hearing, listening out into the otherwise silent night. It became rapidly louder, as if something was flying at high speed between houses on both sides, along the village street.

Having reached a peak, just as rapidly the noise started to fade again and, eventually, it ceased altogether. Whatever it was that was flying, had flown past the house, Karyn thought. Must have been a flock of birds or something. No. There were no birds which had that kind of size or flocking behaviour, and in any event, they would not be flying at this hour of the night. Unless - they were a gang of large owls? Possibly…

The house was thrown into dead of night silence once more, and she settled back into her novel. Moments later, Karyn heard the combined screams of what must have been a hundred stallions coming from the barn stables at the back, as if some catastrophic attack was launched on the entire herd simultaneously.

'Hey, honey. Wake up! Something's attacking the horses,' she shouted, as she nudged her husband from side to side.

'Hmm…What?' He asked, still half asleep.

By now, virtually the whole village had been awakened by the most horrendous noises of agony coming from the stables. Karyn and her husband reached the barn closest to them at the back of their house, and were greeted by the most gruesome sight imaginable. The stables were awash with blood and the carcasses of horses lay littered across the hay-covered floor, in every single stable. Skeletal remains of their heads were scattered around separate and apart from the bodies to which they belonged. It seemed as if some creature or creatures of incomprehensible ferocity and viciousness had slaughtered every single horse in cold blood, and eaten the last ounce of flesh available...

The alternate dimensional plane where wolf angels roamed the interstellar night had momentarily intersected the material plane of starship dwellers, and the phantom beasts took full advantage of the overlap. Although they had no control over the timing of such intersections when the two realities of space-time merged, they did possess the necessary intelligence to coordinate the attack. On this occasion, their strike was particularly well timed and their archangel leader had decided, in the given circumstances, they could do more damage by slaughtering the vast horse population as opposed to injuring a few humans.

That incident marked a truly dark day in the life of the Colacos, as indeed the rest of the people in the farming complex's small village community. With horses removed from their livelihoods for the foreseeable future, until such animals could be reintroduced from the DNA bank, their futures took a huge turn in direction going forward.

9. The energy barrier

Credit: www.headstartproject.org

Caroline rushed into the Med's foyer, where Crista and Chang had been discussing the deepening crisis across the interior. Most of the flurry of reported nightmare attacks now came from rural areas outside of Utopia, where a permanent end of nights policy could not be implemented.

'It worked!' She said and beamed, dashing into the reception room to grab a printed chart.

Chang cocked his eyebrows. 'What worked?' He said.

'This. The electromagnetic resonance seemed to dampen the effect more than ninety nine point nine per cent,' she said, holding out the chart on the clipboard.

Chang thought for a moment.

Meanwhile, Crista took the clipboard from her hand and studied its findings.

'What about subjectivity? Are you certain the results weren't specific to one patient?' He asked.

'Yep. First night, we tried it with just Irene. On the

second night, we had the same set up around the bedside of Razia, her friend. The results showed a virtually identical drop-off in nightmare induced energy patterns. Even better, those results were with the bedroom lights turned off completely, for both subjects,' Caroline explained, enthusiastically.

'In pitch black? No wolf dreams?' Chang asked, with a tone of amazement.

'No bad dreams,' Caroline said.

She could not help chuckling at the funny way Chang referred to the dream creatures.

'Well. I haf to say, well done!' Chang praised. 'So if electromagnetic resonance keep the wolf out, how do we implant starship-wide mechanic for such device?' He asked.

Crista could see the bigger picture.

'Technically, it should be feasible. The energy ripples created by the electromagnetic field appears to interfere with that which the wolf angels require in order to form their presence in the nightmares. So all we need to do is somehow scale up the size of this field, install it around the ship, and we kiss our angel friends goodbye,' he said confidently.

'Just how, exactly?' Chang asked, 'We would need something across six hundred square kilometres, if to properly safe the inside of this ship.'

'Instead of installing it on a 'per household' basis and activating it around the bed of each person whilst sleeping, why not install such a shield all the way around the vessel on the outside?' Crista offered.

'We haf to think how vast the outer surface area of ship really is? And the cosmic ray exposition would be lethal on the crew doing installation,' Chang said, quizzically.

Caroline had an idea. 'Perhaps we don't have to,' she said. 'Heck, if we could find out whether or not these things can come and go through the solid body of the ship, then it may be feasible to focus on windows on the various observation decks, and just seal those.'

Joey had taken the day off from his normal duties in the control room. He had been asked by a panel of the MMC to collaborate with a colleague from the Manufacturing & Robotics Facilities in the Lower Province, to research all options for manufacturing electromagnetic generators and adapting repairbots to carry out their installation around the starship.

He went to the technology research library building in central Utopia, where Joynal Simmons, the manufacturing director, was waiting to meet up.

'We do not have much time. The periastron passage is predicted soon, and the nightmares are rapidly intensifying,' Simmons said, in a serious tone.

He pulled out a paper chart from the file in his hand and laid it out flat on the table. It looked badly creased and depicted a complex orbital diagram, showing the complete configurations of all the planetary bodies as they moved in relation to the multiple suns of Alpha Centauri, along with tick-marks that indicated time lines.

'Here, this is in a bad state as it's the only working copy I've got, but it will give you a better visual on things,' Simmons said.

Joey examined the chart.

'Yeah, now I remember. I was at the DSTF the other

day. According to Dr. Azura's precise mathematical calcs, the two primary suns of Alpha Centauri are due to pass their closest approach point to one another in just a few months from now. That's when the wolf angels will really get the highest boost in their nightmare inducing energies.'

'Yes but remember, it's also a non-linear relationship; the energies are increasing at a geometric rate. Exponentially, in fact. This means that every day that passes—every hour—they are getting stronger, and *this* periastron passage is unlike any other before. The wolf angels are in a heightened state of alert, and they know we're about to put up a defensive shield intended to bar them out permanently.'

Following a short briefing that outlined what needed doing, the two men got to work, spending several hours looking through the electronic archives and making notes that would contribute towards a full research dossier.

In the late afternoon, Joey was not least surprised when his father walked into the first floor, open plan area of the library. He was probably doing more 'Earth studies', Joey thought.

'Hello son. Strange to see you here, how are things?' The wide faced, grey haired man beamed.

'Fine, dad. I'm doing some urgent research on electromagnetic generators,' Joey said softly, to keep the noise down in the quiet study area.

'Electromagnetic generators? What on earth for?'

Joey grinned.

'Dad! Don't you watch the news programs any more these days? These generators are going to keep out the wolf angels syndrome.'

'Yeah, I heard summat about that. Sounds important. Well, I just happen to be doing a fair bit of research myself on the old ship building technology they hired to put together the *Princess* in what they used to call a 'high Earth orbit' back then. Anyway, that's enough about technology. So how is the lovely Alcyone then? Do I hear any wedding bells soon?'

Joey smiled. 'She's good. Listen, I'll talk to you after.'

'Okay, I'll leave you in peace.'

Joey's father took the seat at the work station behind him, and pulled up a host of historic information on a screen. He was a well known advocator and enthusiast of Earth Studies, a subject that was rarely taught these days in the school curriculum. It was naturally dedicated to all about planet Earth, the starship's ancestry and its technological and cultural heritage from that far away place.

Folks in the first millennium of the voyage had placed great emphasis on knowing all about mother Earth and maintaining an ongoing telecoms link that kept everyone informed about the ever changing fortunes of civilisations at both ends. Towards the end of the second millennium, however, the devastation that the Earth had suffered from the ongoing Great Ice Age, had made it progressively more difficult to keep communications flowing in a meaningful way.

As the centuries passed by, the so-called round trip 'light time' for laser signals to cross the vast distance separating the ship from planet Earth, stretched out into months rather than weeks. Those kinds of ever extending delays did not help either. Typically, the navigation team on the ship would send a recorded message, comprising voice, data and video images using interstellar, pulsed-laser optical telemetry from the main control room. Then, assuming the signals got through without suffering too much interstellar extinction along the way, a few months later, they would receive a weak signal back from Earth by similar means. It would then take a huge amount of time and effort to process and decode the signal into something that made sense to anybody. The whole set up thus made staying in touch, more and more painful.

And so the subject of Earth Studies gradually lost its popularity with subsequent generations. The consensus seemed to be that why should anyone bother to look back toward an archaic civilisation on a world that had fallen from grace largely due to mis-management by its own inhabitants? So much so, that these days, anybody who spent too much time delving over old Earth history, was viewed as a 'fuddy daddy'. Joey's father was, unfortunately, very much in that category.

'Psst...Joey! Did you know, when they initially boarded the nine hundred passengers for this mission, the whole operation was carried out under extreme government secrecy? And that the US president put his entire clan onboard as members of the MMC for a succession of dynasty rule?' He spoke in a half whisper, trying to keep the noise down in the silent study area.

'Well, how else could they have done it? I mean choosing a handful of people for this idyllic ark, on their way to paradise, escaping a dying planet of ten billion.

Come on dad!' Joey was obviously trying to concentrate on his work.

'All right son. Here's another. I bet you did not know that the AIDS epidemic had become *airborne*, and it had reached the colonists on the Moon and on Mars, through terrorism and security breaches. Eventually, they had to pull the plug on those colony settlements in favour of the *Centauri Princess* project in 2250 AD.'

'Okay, I did not know that. Those are fascinating facts, I'm sure. But please can we talk about them another time?'

'Sorry son. I'll leave you in peace now. But you must promise you'll come round next weekend. Your mom wants to see Alcyone there too.'

'Okay. I promise we'll be there.'

Joey continued his research in peace, as his father left the library.

The *Centauri Princess* had been originally assembled in a high Earth parking orbit of roughly circular geometry, just over twenty eight thousand miles above, and co-planar with, the equator. The starship's fully constructed outer, bullet shaped dimensions measured approximately twelve miles long by seven miles wide. This meant vast payloads had to be lofted up using unmanned heavy-lift rockets. The process of accumulating ready built parts in high Earth orbit, that would simply slot into place, called for some ten to fifteen rocket launches per week on average, over the entire twenty five year long program. A total of some thirty separate launch sites, scattered across various geographic locations around the globe, were used for sending the myriad of starship parts skyward. Having that number of launch sites gave the project flexibility to supply the construction program on a continuous basis, by launching into various orbital geometries that minimised the waiting time between successive launch windows. Like the pieces in a jigsaw puzzle, partially autonomous robots (orbital 'assembly-bots') were then piloted from ground control rooms to carry out assembly of the ship into its basic, outer framework. That initial phase of the construction program required no human crews to be physically present in orbit, way outside the protection cushion provided by the Earth's *Van Allen radiation belts.*

The starship exterior body parts were made from precision engineered CST (short for carbon-steel-titanium)—an advanced materials science technology that offered the highest in durability and tensile strength of any metallic alloy known to man at the time. The framework built from this ultra-strong alloy, was deemed adequate enough for the starship to be able to withstand micrometeoroid impacts on a voyage spanning at least 50,000 years into the future, i.e. the full duration of the mission. During construction, interim tests had amply demonstrated the structure to be capable of containing an outward-pushing, total pressure of one atmosphere and accommodating the huge, inertial stresses of rotation to generate one-g of Earth gravity throughout the cylindrical interior.

To achieve an average thickness of one kilometre all the way around the body of the vessel, the outer CST framework was then 'padded' over, i.e. overlaid with rocky asteroidal material, which had been robotically processed and transported in from engineering facilities operating in the asteroid main belt and lunar orbit.

Finally, to allow trees and vegetation to grow across the interior, this padding was further overlaid with natural Earth soil to an average depth of fifty or so metres in all parts of the cylindrical interior - barring the Great Front and Rear Walls, which had no artificial gravity and therefore had to be simply left bare.

The *Centauri Princess*, the grandest engineering and technological achievement in all human history, weighed in with a mass comparable to that of a small asteroid or even a miniature moon; one estimate in fact equated it's gross weight to the equivalent of ten per cent of the mass of Deimos, the smaller moon of Mars.

Zakarov was at the vast complex that made up the Manufacturing & Robotics Facilities (MRF), in the Lower Province. In contrast to the starship's broader interior, where a casual glance at the landscape, streets and houses would have given one the impression of a very basic, eco-friendly society that had achieved very little technological advancement over that of twenty third century Earth, here at the MRF things appeared vastly different.

The structure of the entire complex was metallic and it had a silvery shine throughout, with vast, single storey technology plants laid out across hundreds of acres of land. These housed the most advanced manufacturing equipment, industrial robots and raw materials ever known to mankind. It was here, where every single component that made up the broader infrastructure of the *Centauri Princess*, from underground recycling drivers to cryogenic fuels for the space shuttles and the navigation platforms to fleets of advanced repairbots, could all be manufactured and replaced as and when such a task became necessary.

On a voyage spanning hundreds of centuries, it was almost inevitable that a given piece of hardware making up the infrastructure of the ship would, at some point or other, require repairing or replacement. So the MRF was fully stocked on initial departure from Earth, with all the necessary spares to meet such needs, available onboard. The mining of metallic ores found underneath the surface ice of Oort cloud planetoids, was to be used for replenishment as the hardware stock got gradually used up along the journey.

'Tell me something Joynal. I know we've done every study feasible to ascertain this, but are we absolutely certain the wolf angels can *only* come and go through the glazed outlets of the ship?' Zakarov asked, as he was shown around one of the MRF plants by Joynal Simmons, director of manufacturing.

'As creatures of 'pure energy', it's the only conclusion we could reach. As you know, the body of the *Princess* averages one whole kilometre in gross thickness all around, and is never thinner than five hundred metres at any given point. Even high energy gamma rays, fired from one of our most powerful blasters - at close range, could not penetrate that kind of depth,' the manufacturing chief explained.

They moved on to a section of the plant where two repairbots were seen hovering in mid-air, several feet above the shiny floor. They were surrounded by a team of four men, dressed in lab-style white uniforms, who were carrying out testing and evaluation.

'Those two being adapted for the operation?' Zakarov asked, pointing to the larger than normal looking repairbots.

'They are indeed. We are preparing a total of four such units to carry out the electromagnetic generator installations. It's a task and a half. In our feasibility studies, Joey and I had to look at everything, from autonomous thruster control under zero-g to complete shielding from cosmic radiation of all the electronics,' Simmons explained.

The two repairbots were significantly larger in terms of physical size, reflecting the extra accessories, such as fuel tanks and equipment tooling that they needed to carry.

'All that work would have been unnecessary, if only we could have installed the energy barriers to operate from *inside* the ship,' Zakarov reflected.

'Sure thing. But as you know, the high voltage electric fields that these things need to generate would burn someone alive, if they walked within twenty feet of an observation window. To install them on the inside would mean we would be permanently pulling the curtains on all the splendours of our night skies - and *forever*, at that. For future generations, it would be a bit like living inside a windowless tin can!' The two men smiled at the thought, as they walked on.

'The generators are being manufactured over in that section.'

Simmons pointed across the plant to a far location, criss-crossed by conveyor belts flowing along in various planes and overlooked by assembly line robots that hovered above them. The plant was noisy, with a myriad of sounds coming from a range of mechanical and electronic devices in all directions. Zakarov hated the noise. There were electronic sparks, metal grinding, polishing, drilling, etching, scribing...just about every sound one expects inside a hi-tec technology plant in full operation, was there.

Simmons led the way, and they boarded an elevator that took them to the roof top, where it was less noisy and much easier for them to talk.

They stood in the open area, marvelling at a view of the surrounding landscape, as they mulled over things. Zakarov had seldom visited the MRF, and certainly never had the opportunity to see things from the perspective of one of its plants' roof tops. He eyed the intricate, metallic structures stretching out in all directions across the curved landscape. Afternoon sunshine poured down from the myriad of miniature suns, seen going up into the distance.

Looking six miles overhead, through a break in the flaky clouds, an aerial vista of central Utopia was presented showing the *diamond bridge* in its full daytime sparkle, with Eridanus flowing underneath. Such a spectacle was possible to view from here, since the MRF and Utopia were positioned diametrically opposite one another along the cylindrical interior of this exotic world. Zakarov fully admired the 'city and river in the sky' scene as he stared up, somewhat fixated by the wonder. He scanned the sky over to the left, looking for a tiny brownish coloured dot that marked his suburban town house. And there it was. His already strong sense of pride in owning the place was further inflated now; seeing his 'castle in the sky' from this vantage point was indeed a rare and privileged sight.

'We need the generators and the bots delivered to the EVA bay within two days. Are you sure you will be able to meet this schedule?' He said, glancing back down.

'I'll make it a day and a half for you Zakarov, if I can. My colleagues and I are working round the clock,' Simmons assured him, as the tour came to a close.

Zakarov returned to MMC headquarters in Utopia, for a briefing with senior officials.

The roll-out of the electromagnetic generator installations was to be handled manually from inside the cockpit of space shuttles, by utilising vacuum-adapted repairbots to do the physical work. This was the most effective way to minimise direct crew exposure to cosmic radiation and any impact from interstellar gas and dust, to which they may have been otherwise subjected whilst working out in the hazardous environment of deep interstellar space.

The extravehicular activity (EVA), dubbed 'Operation Energy Barrier', comprised four separate space shuttles. They were to be launched from the *Princess'* EVA bay in the Lower Province, and each one was to be piloted by an astronautical engineer who would manually guide the installations. Joey, Zakarov, Simmons and Azura were all selected as pilots for the task.

Several well wishers, made up of family, friends and relations had turned up at the EVA bay to see the men off. The mood was very bleak and sombre. Minds were filled with apprehension about sending loved ones out into the daring environment of space in this dark, eleventh hour of the climaxing wolf angels syndrome.

Alcyone was there, wishing that Joey had not been picked for this bold operation. As far as she was concerned, all EVA flights were grossly 'off-limits' in her world, and she was very sad to see him go. Childhood memories of the tragic accident that had taken the lives of her parents on a similar flight all those years ago, flooded back to her. Joey meant everything to her at this moment in her life, and any thoughts of losing him struck like a hammer blow to the heart.

'I promise, I'll be fine,' he reassured.

She was deeply distressed, and tears rolled down her cheeks.

'I love you Joey. If only...'

Emotions became too overwhelming. She pulled out a handkerchief from the pocket of her tunic.

'I wish you didn't have to go,' Alcyone said, as she dried her eyes.

'I love you too sweet heart, but it's what I have to do.'

They kissed. It was a sad kiss, but it symbolised the unmistakable promise of many unfulfilled hopes and dreams yet to come. Alcyone mentally went over a prayer that she had learned especially for the occasion, begging for his safe return.

'It won't take longer than a few hours, and then I'll be back. I give you my word,' he said.

They hugged one more time. She clung to him like glue.

Joey put on his helmet and headed for the door leading out to the airlock chamber, where the shuttle craft were parked. He looked back at her, briefly. A hint of cheer was returning to her face and she managed to force a weak smile.

Once they had been manoeuvred to specific points around the vast, outer body of the ship where observation windows required sealing, the shuttles were anchored to their work points using specially designed tethers. This made the visual guiding of repairbots in their tasks all the more easier, as the ship, the shuttle craft and the repairbots, all rotated in synchronisation with the starship's artificial gravity spin. For purposes of identification and referencing, each space shuttle in the operation had been given a specific number. Thus, Zakarov's—him being the operation's commander— was number one, Joey's was number two, Simmons' number three and Azura's number four. Each of the four shuttle pilots also had command of a repairbot, that would carry out the manual task of installing the electromagnetic generator.

Sat inside the cockpit of space shuttle number two, Joey was perspiring. Not because it was all that hot inside the cabin. He was sweating partly from the mounting tension of the moment, and partly because he just remembered he was still wearing his astronaut helmet. Unclipping its seal with his gloved hands, he removed the bulky component of his spacesuit, placing it on the seat beside him. There was no further need for it once he had passed the airlock chamber and boarded the shuttle; its cockpit cabin was of course fully pressurised with breathable air.

He guided Number 72, the particular repairbot that was allocated to him, to its first location on the vast outer surface of the ship. Based on the roll-out plan briefed to him by Zakarov earlier, Joey's first assignment was to seal one of the three glazed windows looking out of the Lower Province's observation deck. He remembered this was where Alcyone mostly encountered the wolf angels in her own particular nightmares. I shall soon put a stop to that, he thought, as he worked away with dogged determination.

Electromagnetic field generators needed to be securely welded onto the metallic outer body of the ship if they were to serve as effective energy barriers against intruding wolf angels—continuously—for the astonishingly long, forty five thousand years of remaining mission time. That is of course, forty five thousand years of mission time sailing in the darkness of the cosmic night; the remaining three thousand years (to take the total projected mission time to fifty thousand years) would be spent in the brighter neighbourhood of the Alpha Centauri system itself. In theory, operating as beings of pure energy, the interstellar-sweeping part of wolf angels could not function properly within that zone, since they would have problems with the excessive radiation exposure from the three suns.

Number 72, as with its three other robotic colleagues in this operation, was fully equipped with the necessary engineering tools and welding gear, and carried out its tasks extremely skilfully. It did not really need that much guidance from Joey, as its tasks were well rehearsed from in-house simulations done in the Manufacturing & Robotics Facility, prior to the EVA.

Once the generators were installed on opposite sides of the rectangular window, Joey used the shuttle's control console to instruct Number 72 to perform a test. This was confirmed satisfactory, as the strength of the electromagnetic field and its effectiveness in covering the full surface area of the window, was evaluated. Next, in line with the work plan dictated by the roll-out schedule, he commanded the repairbot to move to the second observation window; the same process was to be repeated there, to ensure that particular path of entry for cosmic wolf angels was also fully sealed.

This process was continued by the four men for the next few hours, working in close coordination with one another from inside their individual shuttle craft. They progressively manoeuvred their vehicles, moving from one work point to the next, toward safeguarding all fifteen windows on the starship exterior that had some form of glazed exposure to the black cosmic night.

Inside his house on the edge of the Black Forest, Yurchenko was in his meditative state once more, sitting in the dark room, under candle light with eyes closed. The air was filled with a chemical scent and thick smoke, coming from the incense sticks that glowed red. He saw a murky scene, as an image started gradually forming in his mind's eye. The scene became sharper, its features more pronounced, and he eventually recognised what it was. The *Centauri Princess* was floating in space before him, seen from the outside, set against the backdrop of the cosmic night. Then, as the starship gradually rotated, one by one, he saw the four space shuttles looking like tiny white dots set against the backdrop of the colossal ship's dark body. They were anchored to their individual work points as their occupants coordinated the energy barrier installations.

In this particular session, Yurchenko had this strange sensation in the background all along—at the very edge of his mystical abilities—that something else was somehow there too, watching over the four men as they carried out their work. It was more than just a feeling. A foreboding premonition, in fact, which he did not like, but felt powerless to be able to do anything about.

Too late. It had to be *them*.

Without warning, the wolf angels swooped in like birds of prey and targeted one of the shuttles anchored to the starship. The image in Yurchenko's mind's eye grew larger and magnified the targeted shuttle as the merciless beasts descended down towards it, faster and faster. He realised that what he was witnessing was somehow a graphic animation of the mounting assault, *seen through the eyes of the archangel in the pack - the leader himself...*

Rujina was at Shirin's house in Midsummer Crescent. The two women were in the lounge, keeping an eye on the television coverage of Operation Energy Barrier, aired live over the interactive screen. An atmosphere of gloom and deep apprehension hung in the air, mirroring the same right across the broader interior. Rujina was feeling more nervous today than ever before, since the start of this whole crisis.

'I wish they'd hurry up about it. This thing's been draggin' on for nearly three hours,' she said.

Shirin was a lot more composed, and took the situation in her stride. She was feeding Cutie some millet seeds, as the budgerigar looked decidedly hungry. It rapidly pecked away at the yellow feeding bowl placed inside the cage.

'Well, you know what they say: 'a watched kettle never boils'. I guess you should give it a break,' Shirin said.

'I still can't figure it out. Why—'

Rujina could barely start the next sentence, when the afternoon sunshine coming through the lounge's window was suddenly cut out. The house was plunged into darkness for a couple of seconds, before re-brightening to full daylight strength again. Something was affecting the starship's power supply, and the miniature suns outside were playing up.

'What was *that* all about?' Shirin said, concerned.

'I don't know. But I'm not gonna wait to find out! I'll go and fetch the girls.'

Razia and Irene had been playing out in the garden at the back. The overriding concern on both women's minds at this moment was for their safety. Recognising the importance of the occasion and focusing all attention toward Operation Energy Barrier, the MMC had declared this day to be a 'no school' day.

Rujina hurried toward the kitchen. Before she could reach it, the daylight outside blinked on and off a couple of times again, and went dead altogether. This time, it stayed that way and the interactive TV screen winked out, too. The house was plunged into the blackest of black, pitch darkness. Cutie screamed as loud as it could, becoming restless inside the cage as Shirin walked away.

Responding to the situation at hand, repairbot Number 232 whizzed into the lounge, having instantly turned on its torch beam to help illuminate its way.

'I'll switch to backup power,' it said, and glided toward the home's emergency power control unit, located in the kitchen.

The lounge's lights came on, as the repairbot restored backup power to the interior of Shirin's home.

'You're a life saver, Number 232,' Shirin shouted. 'Now let's go and get Razia and Irene.'

Her and Rujina went out into the garden, which was still plunged into pitch blackness, where it had been bathed in mid-afternoon sunshine only moments earlier. As they looked out, the landscape right across the curved interior of the miniature world echoed back a darkness, far darker and more sinister-looking, than the darkest nights ever witnessed by either of them before.

'Razia! Irene! Girls, can you hear me? Where are you?' Shirin shouted into the darkness. Her own voice faintly echoed back from the silent landscape.

No answer from either of the two girls.

Rujina called out.

Still no answer.

They sent Number 232 on a search and rescue flight, hoping that the little robot could locate the two girls using its super-bright torch beam, as it carried out an aerial reconnaissance of the long garden, going all the way out to the lake.

It scanned the scene for a few minutes, angling its torch beam downward and hovering up and down the length of the extensive garden, without shedding any light on the missing girls.

As they stood in anxious anticipation, surroundings only dimly illuminated by the lighting coming from inside the house, tears rolled into Shirin and Rujina's eyes. Maternal instincts were intensely at play, and both of them automatically began to fear their worst imaginable nightmares coming true. Drowning in the lake was firmly ruled out, as both girls had earnt swimming certificates, having excelled in recent competitions held at Redwood Junior School.

'It's all my fault. I should never have let them out...Not today...' Rujina said, sobbing loudly.

'How the heck were we to know?' Shirin said, wiping her eyes.

Rujina found it hard to convince herself if all of this was genuinely real or she was just having another bad dream; the whole sequence of events were passing way too quickly.

Just then, they heard a series of faint, pulsating sounds coming from the black sky overhead, toward the left. Number 232, hovering in the distance, heard the sounds too. It projected its powerful torch beam in that direction, to help illuminate the scene.

Rujina and Shirin were never to forget the utterly horrific sight which greeted them.

The five wolf angels were flying above the house at speed. And gripped within the clawed hands of two of them, like eagles carrying their prey, were the two missing girls. Both very much alive, wriggling about and crying out for help.

'Oh my good lord...' Shirin said, and screamed loudly.

Rujina fainted. She collapsed onto the floor in a panic

attack, gripped by the sheer terror of the scene.

By now, Shirin's neighbours, from houses on both sides, had rushed out and were looking to climb over or break down portions of their garden fences to try and get to the two terror-stricken women. They were too late to do anything about the lost children though, as the wolf angels swooped up, disappearing into the black sky carrying the two girls as live captives, never to be seen or heard from again...

Several minutes later, the miniature world's power supply was restored back to normality, as afternoon sunshine resumed across the interior.

The fleet of twenty two space shuttles presently in service on the *Princess*, were a lot more advanced in their futuristic design compared to today's space shuttle orbiters operated by NASA, here in the early twenty first century. They had bullet-shaped profiles, with tiny wings and metallic bodies which were built from heavy CST alloy, that gave them enhanced safety features. A crew of up to eight could be accommodated in the pressurised cockpit cabin, and the system was fully autonomous in its piloting, with manual override if it were needed.

Sitting back within the cockpit of his own shuttle, totally unaware of the drama going on inside the starship, Zakarov applied small amounts of pulsed thrust via its attitude control engines. He began to position his vehicle for a round the ship inspection, now that Joynal Simmons was signalling that the last of the fifteen observation windows was being sealed, on the opposite side of the ship. Since he had led the EVA as commander, Zakarov would be the one to perform a three hundred and sixty-degree fly around of the giant ship, to examine in summary level detail the complete installation.

He increased his separation, gaining altitude above the starship's outer surface, so as to obtain a wider field perspective. As the *Centauri Princess'* outer wall rotated underneath him, at a rate of some five hundred miles per hour, it constantly brought fresh surface features into view. Having withstood two thousand years of interstellar micrometeoroid bombardments, the CST-alloyed metallic body appeared pockmarked by a myriad of tiny craters, resembling those often seen on the face of an asteroid or a small moon of one of the giant outer planets within our own solar system.

As Zakarov's shuttle glided in the black vacuum, he was mesmerised by the panoramic scene presented before him through its cockpit windows. The artificial miniature world rotated silently underneath, with the black interstellar night over its horizons seen littered with Milky Way starfields. They were rich in exotic and colourful nebulae, that would have been the dream scene of any astronomy enthusiast back here on Earth today. The perpetual night skies of interstellar space were seen here under true 'dark sky' conditions, that no location within our own solar system could ever have provided. No glares from the Sun, no full moons to wash out the fainter stars, no Zodiacal light, no bright planets...just the nearby stars in their colourful sparkle and the eternal glow of the Milky Way shining all around.

The starship's rotation presently brought into view a

distinctive structure that Zakarov instantly recognised. It was the large communications dish that had been used in the past for two-way coms with Earth. In its design, it was basically a parabolic dish with an aluminised surface that acted like a mirror, serving to converge laser beams to a focal point above its centre. The sensitive detector, erected on a pole that ran through the central axis of the dish, was wired to the Navigation and Control Complex in Utopia, via CPC's internal networks. The interstellar telecom dish was of course now a redundant piece of hardware, no longer requiring any servicing or maintenance since the navigation team had been forced to abandon all contact with Earth, several decades earlier.

With further rotation of the ship, Zakarov suddenly caught sight of something moving in the corner of his eye. He lifted his head up, peering over the dark horizon ahead. That was when he witnessed the aftermath of the vicious attack, which Yurchenko had sensed in his mystical ritual. In the distance, he saw space shuttle number four drifting aimlessly as it was sent into a rapid spin. It had somehow managed to detach itself from its anchored work point, its tether broken and stretching out into space like a piece of rope.

'Dermot! What the hell do you think you're doing?!' Zakarov shouted over the radio link, half expecting an answer.

No reply.

'Dermot, please respond.'

Still no answer.

Zakarov felt totally helpless, as no contingency had been built into the EVA plan for this kind of emergency and no rescue efforts were possible. With the starship cruising at close to sixty thousand miles per hour, it was only a matter of minutes before the shuttle would be left behind.

The runaway shuttle continued its wild, high speed gyrations as it gradually drifted further and further out into black interstellar space...

'Our men were vulnerable out there and the wolf angels knew it. They had the upper hand, and we had no choice but to be at their mercy for those crucial few hours. Tragically, we've lost one of our space shuttles. It was unfortunately, number four, piloted by Dermot Azura.' Zed Lincoln reported over the live television coverage of the nail biting operation.

He was still unaware of the loss of the two girls from Midsummer Crescent, and made no mention of their missing status.

He continued, 'All three remaining shuttles are now speedily returning to the EVA bay, having sealed all fifteen observation windows. Aside from the tragic loss of a life, which we deeply regret, Operation Energy Barrier has been hailed a complete success.'

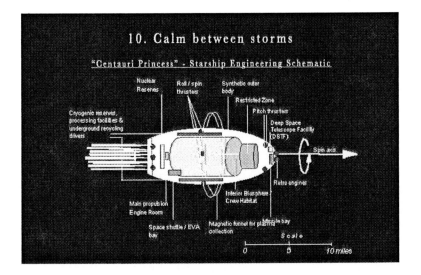

10. Calm between storms

"Centauri Princess" - Starship Engineering Schematic

Four weeks later

The bell at the top of Utopia city centre's clock tower struck seven times, and Zakarov realised he was going to be late in picking up Caroline on his way to the Launch Day ball. He raced Betty at seventy five miles per hour over the *diamond bridge* in the late afternoon sun. Dark shades shielded his eyes, polarising the dazzling colours thrown out with refracted rays. The road ahead shone like a prism as if he were driving through the inside of a polished crystal held up to the sun; diamond railings on both sides still glowed with intensity, even though local 'sunset' was now only about an hour away.

He pulled into Inertia Drive and brought Betty to a sharp halt, half on the sidewalk, in front of Caroline's house. She signalled she'll be out in just two ticks. While he sat there feeling impatient, he stared out toward the road in front. About twenty or thirty feet ahead, something glinted at him from the dusty concrete tiles on the opposite sidewalk of the derelict street. Its shine shimmered in the rising heat. He yanked open the rover door and went across to take a look. It was a silver necklace with a sapphire-embedded pendant. Probably belonged to a child, he thought.

Caroline was out by now and she made herself comfortable in the front passenger seat of Betty.

'Any idea where this might have come from?' Zakarov asked, handing her the item of jewellery.

Caroline's face gradually dimmed, sharply reducing its sparkling expression as she instantly recognised the necklace.

'Belonged to Irene. Where did you find it?'

'Just there,' Zakarov said, as he positioned himself in the driving seat.

Vivid memories of the little girl's frequent visits to the Med flashed through Caroline's mind.

'They must have flown over this part of town on their way out.'

They drove off, Zakarov steering Betty back towards the city centre.

That day marked the two thousandth anniversary since the starship had left Earth. Following conventions of prior years, Zed Lincoln delivered a presidential speech—a somewhat light hearted presidential speech on this occasion—inside the vast briefing hall of the *Centauri Princess* at the centre of Utopia. He was dressed in ballroom-style clothes and stood on the brightly lit stage, with the bulk of the ship's adult population seated:—

'Ladies and gentlemen, thank you all for attending this year's Launch Day celebrations, where we will draw a line under the second millennium of our successful voyage. It's not every year that we get to party away the two thousandth anniversary, so I feel very proud and privileged to be serving as your president on this very momentous occasion. As I am sure you will all agree, this past year has been an extraordinarily difficult one for us, with all the mayhem that we've encountered. Thanks to the sheer commitment and dedication of our people holding office in key positions, once again we have managed to put the ship back onto a merrily sailing path.' He paused briefly, gathering his lines.

'On reflection, it really is a great shame that we have no further communication links with our counterparts back on Earth, as I'm sure they would really have loved to know about all the great adventures, tragedies and sorrows that we're all enduring on our side, just as much as we would like to have known how they are faring on theirs. Well, I guess that's...*c'est la vie*, as they said...back in some place called 'France' was it? Life goes on. Or something like that, anyway!' He chuckled. 'And on that note, I give you dinner and dance. Please enjoy yourselves!'

There followed a thunder of clapping and joyous cheer from the large crowd that echoed across the briefing hall, where a significant proportion of the starship's 3,000-strong population had gathered. They then gradually drifted into an adjacent hall where there was a grander party set up, with elegant chandeliers hanging from ceilings, free drinks and plenty of vintage music that had been specially selected from classical periods back on Earth. To mark this, the grandest of all occasions, special effects had been created using state of the art electronic lighting, holographic images, music and special screens which all blended together to create a dazzling entertainment atmosphere unlike any other that had been experienced within anyone's living memory.

For those few folks who wanted to delve a little into the historical significance of Launch Day celebrations, there was a screen especially set aside for that purpose. It played back old video footage that showed the bitter state of world affairs, the bloody struggle, the political deceit, chaos and corruption that all raged in the months and weeks leading up to Launch Day. That Day was of course the magic moment when Joseph Lexington finally decided to cut the ropes of the *Centauri Princess* that kept her tied to the harbour, and set sail for the New World.

The night was young. The celebrations were in full swing, and the atmosphere had a thoroughly 'groovy' feel about it.

Caroline was with a tall, dark and rather handsome man that she had met at the bar. He was dressed in a dinner suit, and had thick black hair, and brown eyes. She wore a long, ballroom-style dress that perfectly suited her tall, slender complexion.

'You must come over to the Med one of these days,' she invited, sipping champagne from the glass in her hand.

He smiled, staring into her fiery, topaz-blue eyes.

'We have a tight schedule over in the propulsion

room. But sure, one of these days. Definitely,' he said.

As Zakarov walked past them, looking rather cheery, he winked his right eye at Caroline. She smiled back at him.

'Your boss?' Asked the man.

'No, not really. As a matter of fact, he's just my uncle,' she said and laughed.

Zayna, Crista, Chang, Lucy...along with everyone else from the control room and the Med were at the party, too.

Zayna had fully recovered from her nightmare ordeal by now and she had also ended her short relationship with Sharuk. Alcyone and Joey had big wedding plans lined up - thanks to some pressure from Joey's parents. Meanwhile, Shirin and Rujina both made an effort to take part in the celebrations and attended the party, having only partially come to terms with the incalculable scale of their tragic losses.

The Launch Day celebrations ended shortly after midnight, and Zakarov came home to his isolated town house. As he sat on the sofa flicking through late night TV channels, he pondered over a few thoughts that still lingered in his mind after all these weeks since the conclusion of Operation Energy Barrier.

These wolf angels were so well-evolved, and sufficiently intelligent in their thinking to be able to exploit inter-dimensional worm holes, and coordinate the spread of their evil presence across near infinite distances. Now the *Centauri Princess* was safe. But for how long? What if they found a way around the armour of electromagnetic generators? What was their purpose in taking Irene and Razia as captives? What if the MMC had seriously underestimated their powers and they possessed some other, unknown ways or means of delivering even greater devastation in the future, the magnitude and nature of which no human mind could even begin to imagine? What if…? Zakarov knew he had an ever inquisitive mind. But he also knew when to cut short its wanderings. He put all of those thoughts firmly to rest at the back of his mind where they belonged, and headed straight for the bedroom.

That night, while he slept in the tranquil setting of his suburban home, Zakarov had the longest and most fantasy-filled series of dreams that he could remember in his entire forty years. Amongst them, he experienced the full spectrum of his most treasured childhood fantasies: from beautiful mermaids swimming in the deep oceans of an exotic world…to nymphs riding high on celestial winged horses across moonlit, tropical night skies…to white unicorns roaming freely in the vast, flowery meadows and woodlands of a far away planet that had princes, princesses, castles and gigantic water falls…

With the electromagnetic generators now working away continuously in the background to provide complete protection around the clock, the wolf angels syndrome gradually receded into distant memories in most people's minds. And so the starship residents began to enjoy an episode of calm after the storm.

Then again, that could just as easily be calm *between* storms…

In a remote deck, a few miles outside of the main biosphere and going toward the rear of the ship, there operated a huge nuclear power plant. This was the one and only powerhouse on board, supplying the starship's vast electricity needs on an ongoing basis. Adjacent to the plant, contained within a giant lead-shielded vessel, was the uranium fuel reserves with which the ship had originally departed from our solar system.

Unnoticed by anyone within the MMC, that stockpile of nuclear reserves was now being used up at a faster rate than normal; the electromagnetic generators sealing no less than fifteen observation windows by working around the clock, 24/7, consumed vast amounts of additional power. This could easily make the nuclear reserves less adequate looking into the distant future.

Had they been aware of this fact, starship dwellers would probably have kept their fingers crossed that the *Centauri Princess* will not be plunged into permanent darkness before she reaches Delta's ice world in a few years hence…

THE END

Starship biosphere map

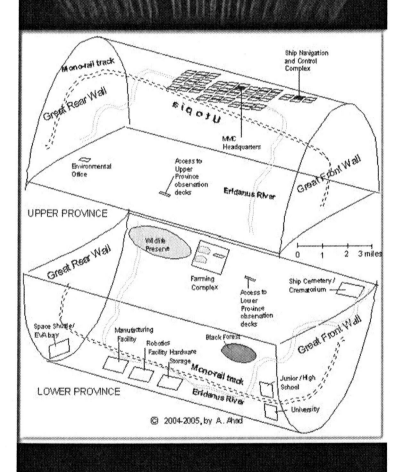

Monorail track

Great Rear Wall

Utopia

Ship Navigation and Control Complex

MMC Headquarters

Environmental Office

Access to Upper Province observation decks

Eridanus River

Great Front Wall

UPPER PROVINCE

0 1 2 3 miles

Wildlife Preserve

Farming Complex

Access to Lower Province observation decks

Ship Cemetery / Crematorium

Great Rear Wall

Space Shuttle / EVA bay

Manufacturing Facility

Robotics Facility Hardware Storage

Black Forest

Great Front Wall

Monorail track

Junior / High School

LOWER PROVINCE

Eridanus River

University

© 2004-2005, by A. Ahad

Printed in the United Kingdom
by Lightning Source UK Ltd.
106414UKS00001B/17